A Little Life

By Joseph Hoskins

A Little Life
By Joseph Hoskins

A writer draws on his experiences and may be influenced to write about what he knows, even when he is conjuring a story of the imagination. The following story is a work of fiction.

Names, places, characters and incidents are the product of the author's imagination. Any resemblance to actual persons, places, or businesses is entirely coincidental.

Dedication

I would like to dedicate this book to the American family. They say, "All families are dysfunctional." The story you're about to read certainly is no exception. Poverty exacerbates dysfunction, although no family is immune.

The characters in this story may remind you of your own family or someone you know. I hope you'll be entertained by what you read.

Joseph Hoskins

Preface

Sometimes in the periods of deepest distress, when cataclysmic events occur, the result of a happy ending can follow when it appears impossible at the time.

Often, the close friends who stand behind you during the hardest times become family, especially when your blood family abandons you.

Friendships have a life. Sometimes a friendship will last only a few years, or as short as a few months. At other times, long-time friendships can die after many years due to changing circumstances and distances between.

If you're lucky, you will have a good friend, family member or other, that will last you until your end days. You are truly blessed if you have one or more friends like this.

The story that follows includes such a friendship.

Forever Poor

Momi bought the accordion
with the rent money.
Her love for her son exceeded her good judgement.
I told her I'd send it all back
within a month.
That was a year ago,
I dare not show my face now.
Dreams die hard, my friend.
Living on scraps found in trash cans
has kept me alive.

"A song for a euro!"
Working the trains from Firenze to Venezia
nets me 11 euros on a good day.

Someday, my dream of success may come true.
But seeing the world from the bottom
has impoverished my soul,
and even though, with the dismal chance of future
riches, I hit the big time,

my spirit shall remain forever poor.

Table of Contents

Chapter 1
My History

I was born during a sandstorm that blistered the tiny cotton plants across most of the high plains of Texas. I started out life small, at 5 lbs. and throughout my growth to manhood, have remained short, and small of stature.

My mom, Missy, was a beauty in her school and her first husband, Ron, was a handsome dude, though a proven loser. Before he left her, she was to bear 3 sons with him, with me being the second of the lot.

Fate sometimes displays its sense of humor which does not prove kind to its victims. My brothers and I did not inherit the genes that would have given us the handsome looks we deserved based on our parents' appearance.

On the contrary, we were all short and cursed with being homely. This unfortunate fact worked to our disadvantage in a world that valued the tall and attractive. We were all to make our way as people do. Of course, mothers of all species love their children, but once we became too big to cuddle, we were pretty much ignored.

With what we're told, we shared the same parents, but look very different from each other, with the only thing in common, were our parents, and being altitude challenged bantams.

After the third son was born, Ron left Mama for greener pastures and sexual variety. He was not ready for a life burdened by supporting a wife and 3 children. That left her in a lurch. The day he walked out of the house is my first and oldest memory.

One day I was visiting Mama and, regrettably, in need of a little cash. If Mama ever had a penny, she would give it to her boys, with only the asking.

I knew she lived on a small, fixed income and, at age 35, I felt guilty about asking for it.

But another wolf was at the door, and she was my last resort.

Someday I plan to surprise her and pay it all back. She would never expect that.

In walked my Aunt Jinks from Arizona, whom I had only seen once or twice in my life. She had driven all the way from Phoenix to visit my grandmother. She dropped by to visit with my mom. She had a daughter close to Mom's age.

I have always been a late sleeper and had just awakened and retrieved my first coffee for the day. I sat and listened while Aunt Jinks was visiting candidly with Mama and seemed to be grilling her.

Aunt Jinks greeted me. "Good morning, little man! Why, aren't you a handsome devil. I'll bet the women want to put you in their pocket and take you home."

"Hi Aunt Jinks." Her remarks no longer bothered me as I considered the source. My grandma told me once that Jinks had a checkered past of her own many years ago.

I listened while she interrogated Mama.

"Missy, What was your reason for marrying the boy's dad at such a young age? I know you weren't pregnant."

"First of all, his name is Ron. No, we did not have sex before I was married," she said. Mama would have killed me. In those days, all her churchy friends began the monthly count from the wedding day to the birth of the first born."

"If the time was less than nine months, they knew that sexual scandal was obvious and yet another young girl with loose morals would begin adult life under the cloud of shame.

"Sometimes they would try to get away with saying they had an eight-pound premature child at 6 months, but it didn't fool anyone." No one who stayed around needed a scarlet letter to remind everyone of their misdeeds. The church ladies did their work."

"Missy, in this day and time, nobody cares about that stuff anymore. More young kids are living in sin than ever before, and having kids too, without being married. Nobody turns a head."

"Now tell me, Missy, did Ron show promise of being a good husband in those young days? Was he a good student in school?"

"No, actually, Ron dropped out of high school before his senior year. His grades were terrible. He didn't seem to care," she replied.

"I see. Well, was he a good family man?" my aunt asked. Did he get along well with his brothers and sisters?"

"No," Mama replied, "his dad kicked him out of the house when he quit high school. They fought constantly. He lived with one friend for a while, then moved in with another. He really didn't have a home. He was kind of a drifter."

"Did he have skills for getting a good job that didn't require an education?"

"No, he chopped cotton and could drive a tractor. He had hoped to earn enough by working for local farmers to buy himself a car."

"He never was able to stay with one farmer long enough to save any money. Eventually, word got out among the farmers that he was lazy and not a good worker. No one around here would hire him."

"What? When you got married, neither of you had a car?" Well, that's starting life behind the eight ball. Let me see if I have this right: Ron was a high school drop-out, he had poor family relations, he had no job and no prospect for one. He was poor and had no car. He must have been a charmer. What made you think you wanted to marry someone like that?"

"Well, we were in love. I had just turned 18 and had graduated from high school. I wanted independence. I decided that I wouldn't be told what to do by anyone and would make my own decisions. Besides, my best friend, Cherry, was engaged to Ron's brother. I didn't want to get married after she did. I felt that it would have taken away from my wedding."

"Why are you asking all these questions? I'd kindly be obliged if you'd change the subject," Mama said.

I could see that Mama was riled and didn't want to be reminded that she had made some bad decisions, especially in front of me.

"I was just curious," my Aunt Jinks said. "Don't get your panties in a wad. I've asked your mama and she doesn't like to talk about it.

"Besides, look on the bright side. If you hadn't married Ron, of course Little Will wouldn't be here today, and I'm thankful for that." Just look at that cute thing over there."

"Will, I don't know why that fat wife of yours left you, but she was a damn fool. Both ex-wives were fools," she said. I know she was trying to cheer me up, but it wasn't working.

Jinks turned back to Mama.

"Missy, I'm a little bit surprised that your mom didn't slap you for going forward with this doomed marriage."

"Actually, she tried to discourage me all the way up to our wedding day. When I put on my wedding veil, her last words whispered to me as a young single girl were: "Missy, you can do better. You can still back out from marrying the lazy bastard.""

"I told her for the last time that my mind was made up and nobody was going to tell me what to do anymore. I know Mom was just looking out for me and wanted me to be happy."

I knew the story of Mama marrying Daddy, but Aunt Jinks' questions bothered me. For the first time in my life, I wondered the same thing about how and why poor Mama got into a doomed relationship like this one.

I excused myself. I wanted a beer, but it was too early in the morning, but more so, I just wanted a quiet place to get away to think.

"Bye, Aunt Jinks. I just remembered that I have to go down to the store to pick up a few things." I hurried into my little truck, hoping there was enough gas to get me across town and back. I found the tiny taqueria empty, except for Merci, who owned the little café and made the tacos and burritos.

"Buenos Dias, Merci, could I have a taco and coffee? I'll be good for it this afternoon."

"Si, Mijo," she answered. "Just pay me before the end of the day. How's your mama?"

"Oh, she is fine. Our Aunt Jinks is visiting from Arizona today. She's at the house now. That's why I'm here." I joked. "I had to get away from all the hen house cackling."

"Stay as long as you want."

The taco was delicious and coffee strong and black, with a little iridescent grease floating on the top. Merci wiped all her cups clean but didn't always use soap. The grease didn't bother me any.

I sat for a long time, refilling my cup every 20 minutes or so, wondering why life had led me back to my childhood home. What Aunt Jinks had been getting at, by grilling my mother, was hard for me to listen to.

If it entertained her to hear the misfortunes of others, she could have gotten just as much satisfaction by questioning me, and not put my poor mother through the ringer. My life is certainly no success story, far from it. *Why do people get a kick out of the misfortunes of others?* I thought to myself.

I graduated from the local high school nearly 20 years ago. Most of the same tired, frustrated teachers that I had then were still at it, praying for the time they could retire and leave the molding of the minds of the backwards little brats to others.

It is sad now to think that I was Mama's fair-haired boy at one time, going to school in the morning and working in the grocery store every afternoon. Living up to a high standard set by others can be one of the hardest things a person can do.

At age 17, I was making payments on a Datsun B210. It was a nicer vehicle than what I have to drive now. Mom was proud of me as well as my Maw Maw, grandmother on my mom's side.

While the cool rich boys in the school were playing football and basketball, I spent my spare time working, carrying out groceries, and stocking the shelves of the store.

"Will, we won't get trucks in today. Can you collect on some bad checks?" Lee, the boss-man asked me.

"Sure," I said. I enjoyed the office work and was surprised that Lee would trust the responsibility of bad debt collections to a high school boy.

Lee was close to the same age as Mama and may have been sweet on her in high school. As it was, he was married, happily as far as I knew, with a couple of little rug rats underfoot.

"Mrs. Bell, this is Will from the Piggly Wiggly store in Podunk. We're holding a check on you marked 'insufficient funds' from the Wilson National Bank. Can you come in today to take care of it?"

"This is who? You sound like a kid. Whatchoo doing calling me about a bad check? I don't 'preciate that one bit," she said. "I'm going to call your boss."

"Mrs. Bell, it was my boss who asked me to call you. You owe us $36.65 for your bad check plus a $3.00 bad check fee. Now if you can come in this week and pick up your check, we'll waive your $3.00 fee.

"That is a good deal. If you don't pick it up before Monday, we're going to take it to the district attorney, and you'll have to deal with him. It will cost you another bad check fee. You would best get in here and pay what you owe us."

"There you go again, you little runt. Don't you go threatening me. Do you know who I am?"

"Yes, you are the one who owes us $36.65 and if you don't come in real soon to pay, you'll have to deal with the district attorney."

"You shut your smarty-pants mouth and maybe I'll come in by Friday, and maybe I won't. That's all I have to say to you." Click!

I wrote "Contacted. Might come in by Friday" on her card and went on to the next check. On and on I continued with pretty much the same results until I reached the end of the stack.

It was back to the soap aisle for me. We also sold lard from the soap aisle. I don't know why lard was on our aisle, but we sold tons of it. Women in those days fried a lot of food.

"Will, you're doing a good job working here in the store. Stay in school, and keep your nose clean, and you'll be running a place like this someday," Lee said to me as I hung my green apron on my peg and started home.

Lee was more disappointed in me than I was in myself the day I got into trouble at the store. Paolo, the meat cutter, and I were outside the store smoking a joint, when Roger, the assistant manager came upon us from out of nowhere.

Roger was a straight arrow; the teacher's pet kind of fellow that most of the other students didn't like. I'm not sure that any of the teachers liked him either, but he was a rule follower. "I'm going to turn you both in," he said. "You could go to prison for what you're doing."

"Oh, you're going to put us in prison for taking a break. Check the handbook. It's in there. Why don't you leave us alone and go back to work. Maybe if you change your tampon, you'll be in a better mood."

Paolo chuckled at my joke.

"You're smoking marijuana and that's against the law. I'm telling Lee." Roger stomped off towards the manager's office.

To be honest, I didn't think Lee would mind too much. There have been times that I was sure that I smelled pot on him.

Roger returned with Lee. "Are you smoking marijuana on the job?" Lee asked. We just stared back at him without offering a reply. "Paolo, go to my office now and wait for me. Will, you are fired. Get your things and leave the store."

"Are you really firing Paolo and me for smoking a joint?"

"No, I am firing you. Paolo is the meat cutter. He will be reprimanded. Now git!"

This was not the first time I was to misjudge a situation. I was in my little Datsun when I remembered that I left my stash of pot in the bathroom. I went back inside.

"Will, why are you back here? I told you that you had to skedaddle."

"I left something personal in the store. I'm just retrieving what is mine."

Lee followed me into the bathroom. "I'll take that! he said. You'll just get into more trouble with it." Lee put it in his pocket.

"What are you going to do with it?" I asked. "It cost me twenty bucks."

"I just might keep it for evidence, just in case the authorities want to see it."

I had the strong feeling that the baggie would never see the evidence room.

I never saw Lee after that scene. I missed working at the store, my friends there and, of course, the income source. There weren't many employment opportunities for teenagers in our dusty little town back then.

Fortunately, I was to graduate soon from high school. I was a strong "C" student at the time and had no money to go to college. My uncle, Charlie, had worked his way up the ladder in management in a chain of cheap furniture stores. He was my mom's brother.

He and Mama were close, and he knew my dilemma of needing a job or risk losing my car due to not being able to make the car payments. Maw Maw, my grandmother, had asked him to hire me after high school. Maw Maw and Paw Paw had farmed in the county all their lives. They knew a lot of people and could ask for favors.

Uncle Charlie didn't care one way or another about my well-being. He was becoming rich and successful in the corporate world. He didn't need trailer trash relatives close to him making him look bad.

He did, however, care for his sister, Missy, my mom. So he promised her he would help me out.

One morning at 10:00, Mama called me, "Will, get out of bed. Charlie's on the phone and wants to offer you a job. Hurry up!"

"Will, this is your Uncle Charlie. Are you still working at the grocery store office collecting bad checks?" My Maw Maw had told him about my job, but not how it had ended.

"No, Uncle Charlie, I recently quit that job because now that I'm out of high school, I'm looking for a career with a brighter future." I thought that sounded good. Would he know I was lying?

"Will, our company has a job opening in Prairie, Texas. You'll have to move, but you will make a good starting salary for a young turk like yourself. You'll be selling furniture, moving freight, and helping the manager. It would be a job with a future. If you do well there, promotions would come and, in time, you could eventually become a store manager.

I dared to dream again. Wow! I thought. What would my low-life loser friends say if they found out that I was a manager in a furniture store, making the big salaries, and maybe even driving a new pickup truck. Hmm...they would want money and to stay with me. I wouldn't tell them.

I returned to reality.

"Uncle Charlie, I am interested in the position. I have a few feelers out in several other places," I lied, "but I can cancel those, and go to work in your store. When do I need to show up for work?" I asked.

"Go to the Prairie store Wednesday at 9:00 a.m. I will introduce you to the store manager, Mr. Platney."

My luck was finally changing for the better. I had just received written notice that they were coming after my Datsun. It wasn't running well, but I didn't want to lose it. This job offer was just in time for me to save losing my car.

Prairie, Texas was an easy two-hour drive away. Mr. Platney was a very old man. His wife worked at the store, too. There were only 4 other employees besides the two of them. She was the buyer and merchandise manager.

He said I could call myself the assistant manager. Wow! An immediate promotion.

"Now Will, you are salaried and that means that you are to come in every day. You will get Sundays and Wednesday afternoons off unless we're short-handed and you have to help get us out of a bind. Your job description is to do whatever I ask you to do, no matter what it is. Do you understand that? You do what we tell you without sass."

"Sure, I understand. I'll do whatever you want. I aim to start a lifetime career here," I answered, trying to sound enthusiastic.

*   *   *   *   *

Merci came by with the coffee pot and filled my cup. She could see that I was daydreaming, and I never noticed her. I just looked down and my cup was full.

"Gracias, Merci. You are the best. I wish I had a mother like you."

"Your mama is a good person. She has worked hard for you boys. Don't ever forget that. Kids these days don't appreciate their parents. That is what is wrong with the country. Sometimes I wish I was back in Guanajuato. Do you want another taco, Mijo?"

"No, the coffee is enough. I think I'll just stay here a while longer."

"You know, Will, I have a sobrina back in Mexico. She is short like you, but a pretty girl. She is looking for a husband. I could fix you up if you like. She is not fat like your other two wives, and she is a good cooker."

"It sounds interesting, Merci, but I want to get back on my feet before I begin looking for another wife. You know what they say, 'A scalded dog thinks all water is hot.'"

"I don't know what you mean. Drink your coffee."

I had no place to go, and all day to get there. I was lost revisiting my past. There I was, not so many years ago, at age 18, an assistant manager already, with dreams. Mama and Maw Maw (my grandmother) were proud of me. I even had business cards made and they handed them out to everyone they knew.

Life went well in little Prairie, Texas. I made several good sales of furniture early on and the manager's wife gave me a necktie to wear every day.

I still had to pick up trash and clean bathrooms, but I looked like the successful young executive. I would follow my uncle's footsteps.

Life went well. I was earning money and paying on my car again. On Sundays, I drove back to Podunk and arrived in time to have dinner with Mama and my brothers.

My brothers' names are Gordon, Otis, and Freddy. Of the four of us, there have been seven marriages. Gordon is on his third wife, two wives have left Freddie, and Otis has never married. I am twice-divorced now, with no prospects nor aspirations to ever tie the knot again.

Of these, only Gordon is still married. Three has been the magic number for him. You have to admit, he didn't give up. After two marriages and two bankruptcies, he has found his soul mate.

I'm happy for him although I've never seen a sadder man than he seems to be now. Fat Gordon was never a pleasant person to be around. He has a voice that gets very high pitched, almost shrill, when he is angry, which is most of the time.

The funny thing is, that when he displayed his anger in the past, he showed life. Now he is always in a funk, like the core of his soul is being eaten away from the inside. Now he has, yet another, fat wife who spends everything he makes. Funny how fate can get you no matter which way you turn.

Freddy actually has a different father. He's a head taller than the rest of us, spanning a full 5' 8" in height. He has gone through two wives, or more accurately, two have gone through him. He lives with Mama and helps to take care of her in her old age.

So, my family's history of marriage does not bode well for my marriage future. Getting married has been easy; staying married, not so much. A settled down life is just not in our genes.

Otis, the "Big O" has never tied the knot. He's had a few girlfriends, but nothing ever worked out enough for him to get to the pulpit. His most recent ladylove broke his nose with an unexpected head-butt. His nose was never reset, and a little off to one side, resulting in his profile that resembles a painting by Pablo Picasso.

But back to my job in Prairie, Texas. Mr. Platney and his wife gave me rave reviews. Our company was growing as Uncle Charlie was instrumental in acquiring furniture stores for Slugs, in some very small towns across Texas.

Mr. Platney told me that he had recommended me for a position of manager in one of the new stores. I noticed that Mabel, his wife, had taken a new interest in me, also. I was to learn, of not the same nature. I didn't think much at the time of her putting her hands on me often.

Early one morning as I was picking up trash hours before the store opened, she was in the back room where we kept the twin mattress.

"Will, have you ever heard that the older the grapes are, the sweeter the wine?"

"No, Mrs. Platney, I haven't heard that. I don't drink much wine."

"Now little Will, the drink is not what I'm talking about. You seem a little slow, so I'll show you, and you can call me Mabel."

I was caught by surprise as old Mrs. Platney proceeded to remove her jewelry and then…. her clothes.

"Hurry up and get undressed, little man, we don't have much time."

"Mrs. Platney, uh, Mabel, I don't think this is a good idea."

"Will, I can see that you are a healthy young man, and you must have needs that all young men have. I have a good feeling that you don't have much going on in your personal life."

"I have those needs, too, and at my age, don't get many opportunities to fulfill them. Now hurry up."

Mrs. Platney, nude now, planted a big kiss on my forehead and pushed my face into her sagging breasts. I gave in, and nature took its course.

I'm not proud of that moment, but I remember that at the time, I had felt guilty for enjoying myself. I have never told anyone about that moment but have never forgotten it.

I feel kind of dirty thinking about it, and it was hard to look Mr. Platney in the eye for a while after that moment.

Time heals all problems, and things were back to normal soon. Every once in a while, Mabel would wink at me when no one else was looking.

I was ready for that promotion. I could not see good times ahead in staying in Prairie any longer than I had to.

It was only a few months later, that I received a rare call from Uncle Charlie.

"Will, I have been getting a lot of reports on what you've been doing there at the store. Do you want to tell me about how things are now?

Oh hell, I thought. *The word is out and I'm going to get fired.* "I'd like to explain my side," I said.

"Your side? What are you talking about? Lighten up little fellah, I'm calling to offer you a promotion. At age 21, you're going to have a store of your own and will be the company's youngest manager."

My heart had been beating so loudly I could hear it. I was breathing hard. With the news, I was finally calming down. Guilt is a stronger emotion than we wish it to be.

"Well, that's great news," I stammered.

"Will, are you feeling all right? You sound a little off."

"Oh no, I feel fine. The good news just caught me by surprise."

"I'm coming on Thursday to introduce the new assistant manager to Kent and Mabel. Make reservations at the best restaurant in Prairie for the five of us. We'll make this a pleasant transition, and the company will foot the dinner bill."

"Yes sir. Will do."

"Will, get back to work and sell some La-Z-Boys. I'll see you Thursday. Bye."

"Bye." I said. He hung up before he could hear my reply.

Dinner was at Applebee's. We reserved a table for five, although the rest of the restaurant was nearly empty.

"I want to sit by my little man," Mabel said.

She was wearing a low cut slinky floral dress by Diane Freis and lipstick that was fire engine red. She made me nervous just sitting beside me while we talked about the best-selling furniture items of the store. At times, I felt a warm toe tickling my leg underneath the table. I was sweating.

Uncle Charlie ordered wine. "Will, do you drink wine, or would you like something else?" For some reason, my face turned shades of red. "You can have a beer if you want."

Charlie later said, "Are you sure that you're all right? No more wine for you."

I was glad when the evening was over. I felt that I was escaping a one-way path to a bad end.

On Monday, I reported to my new store in Stonie, Texas. I was wearing the tie that Mabel gave me. On the inside of the tie was an iridescent smudge of Mabel's red lipstick.

*   *   *   *   *

"Mijo, are you sure you are okay? You been here a long time," Merci woke me from my reminiscing. "You want more coffee?"

The restaurant was filling up now with the lunch crowd and I felt that I had overstayed my time there.

"No, gracias!" I replied. "I have to go work now."

"Oh, you have a job now? That is good news."

"No, Merci, I have to go to work trying to find work. Adios." I smiled as I hurried out the door.

"Will, don't forget about paying for the taco and coffee when your money comes in. Bye"

I drove back to the house. Thankfully, Aunt Jinks was gone. I owed Merci for two meals and was hoping to pay her back today. I didn't know how long my credit would hold out there.

"Where have you been so long, boy?" Mama asked. At 35, I didn't appreciate being called boy, but it was Mama and I needed cash. It wouldn't do to say anything to make her mad.

"Oh, I've been taking care of a few errands," I answered. "What's on your agenda today?"

"We have to go to Uncle Charlie's farm and chop weeds around the house. He and Charmy are going out there for the weekend and wanted the house cleaned up."

"Why do we have to clean it?" I asked. "It seems that he takes advantage of you."

"For the damn money!" she said loudly to make a point, accompanied by a dirty look, I knew she was serious, so I clammed up about it.

"Charlie pays me $200 a month to keep his place cleaned up and clear of weeds. That's a lot in this day and time. I can read your face, Will, that you are a little down on your luck and in need of a little cash. When we finish, you can keep the money."

"I hated myself for accepting the money, but the truth was, I owed all of it in small loans, bills, and to Merci for the breakfasts."

My brothers and I grew up poor. Papa and Maw Maw helped to take care of our needs, but cash-wise, we had nothing. I have to admit, sadly, we were a white-trash family. You'd think that because we never had much money, that we'd be careful with it when we finally begun working and earning more of it. It didn't happen. It is the poor man's curse to spend every coin and bill as soon as he has it.

Saving was a word not in our vocabulary. I hate to think that I reached my financial peak before age 30, but so far, that has been the case.

Uncle Charlie told me, "No one is a failure under age 40. Some men just get a late start in life and then realize their potential in their middle age." I was just thinking of his words when Mama yelled to me.

"Will, what in the hell are you doing? You've been leaning on your hoe for the past 30 minutes. I'm almost finished."

"Oh, I'm sorry. I'll get started cleaning the inside."

I stayed on track after that, and the home was "spic 'n span" for Uncle Charlie. I've never known how he has been so lucky in life. He must have done something illegal.

"I already have his check. He sent it earlier in the week. When we get back to town, I'll sign it over to you."

"Thanks Mama, you don't know how much you've helped me out."

"Will, I know that someday you'll get back on your feet. When I get old and you are making the big bucks, don't forget about your old mama. You can help me out when I need it."

"Mama, I'm going to buy you the biggest house in town."

Mama smiled and a tear came into her eye.

The bank teller seemed to scowl when I cashed Mama's check.

"Will, didn't you have a high paying job working in the furniture stores for your Uncle Charlie? What happened to that job?"

Dammit, did the whole little town of Podunk know about my recent unemployment?

"I left it for better opportunities. I learned the furniture business frontwards and back. I felt that the company no longer had anything more to offer me," I tried to sound blasé.

"Don't worry, I've got several leads. Nope, not worried one bit," I answered.

He smirked at me and handed me the cash. I rushed over to Merci's and paid her what I owed her, with lots of cash left.

"Mijo, did you rob a bank?" she laughed. "Don't you spend all that money in one place. Think about my little niece." I smiled and left.

Tomorrow, I'll get the water and electricity reinstated. Then, I'll find that illusive job that will pay me the riches I deserve. I tried to think positive. I decided to see my Maw Maw and say goodbye to Aunt Jinks.

"There's my little man," Aunt Jinks greeted me. "I'm taking you home with me in the morning. You can keep me company on the road back to Phoenix?"

"Don't tease that boy unless you're serious, Jinks," my Maw Maw said. "He might take you up on it. Will is, how do we say, between jobs right now."

"Will, I'm serious, you come with me and I'll get you situated in Phoenix. Phoenix is a big city now. There are thousands of jobs available for young men like you."

"I've got too many irons in the fire now," I answered.

"What have you got to lose?" she answered. "Neither of those boys you've had by those fat wives live with you, do they? Their mamas don't need to know where you are anyway. Come on if you're coming. You'll love it out there."

I was in a quandary. I had the money for my utilities and to pay a few personal loans. But I could keep the cash if I didn't pay them. It would be a fresh start in a new place—something I've wanted for a long time.

Chapter 2
Moving to Phoenix

"Aunt Jinks, I've decided to go with you. I'm going to my apartment now and pick up a few items. Don't leave without me. I'll be back by 8:00 in the morning. Maw Maw, do you have a big trash bag, and can I borrow the pickup truck for a couple of hours?" I asked.

I hurried to my little efficiency apartment and loaded a few clothes, shoes, and some other items in the trash bag. I was packed and ready to start my new future. I hadn't been this excited about anything in years. I would start a new life out west.

I was back by midnight. I went inside and slept. Maw Maw never locked the doors. I was up before 7:00 a.m. having a final breakfast with my grandmother.

"Maw Maw, can you tell Mama bye for me? I'll be back in a few months with enough cash to get the truck fixed. I promise to take you, Mama, and Otis to lunch at the Dairy Queen for the biggest burger they have. You can bank on that."

"I'll tell her," she promised. "Be careful in the big city. There's a lot of mean people out there."

"Will, we'll be in Ruidoso, New Mexico by lunchtime. I may need you to help me drive," said Aunt Jinks. I get sleepy behind the wheel."

"No problem." I answered. As soon as we were on the road, Aunt Jinks started a conversation:

"Will, what happened to your job with the furniture store? It's none of my business but I'm curious. You had a good position there from what your grandmother told me. We've got a long time on the road, so take your time. I want to hear it all."

"Well, I moved from Podunk to Prairie, Texas, then from Prairie to Stonie, Texas, to manage the little store there. That was 15 years ago. I had been assistant manager at Prairie, Texas. I remember it as it were yesterday." I began telling Aunt Jinks my story, discretely leaving out the part about my tryst with Mabel.

*　　*　　*　　*　　*

I bought a road map and found my way to Stonie. I had all my worldly possessions in the back of my little Datsun.

"Welcome to Slug's Furniture. Why, aren't you a sawed-off little feller?" These were the first words spoken to me when I arrived in town.

The store was smaller than the one in Prairie. The office had a female middle-aged manager who did the books, deposits, and reports. Her husband sold furniture and did the re-stocking duties and store clean-up. They had an overweight daughter, close to my age, who worked their days off and helped in the office.

We sold mattresses, sofas, lounge chairs, lamps, and a few wall hangings. The store was small, but profitable and well run.

Uncle Charlie had set me up on a bonus system that was based on the store profit. Whatever the profit was, I was to receive 10 percent.

I never thought about the profit or the bonus until the end of my first year. When I got a check sent to my home, it caught me by surprise. I went out and bought a new color TV.

The office manager's daughter was a plump girl who worked in the store. Her name was Tara. She was my age. She had a nice smile. Somewhere in that moon-pie face was an attractive girl that one could see if they had a good imagination.

I don't think she had many prospects for dating. She put her energies into her work. I imagined later that she saw me as a potential way out of her dusty little town of Stonie.

Everyone was nice to me, and the store pretty much ran itself. I wore the tie every day that my former employer had given me. Life went well.

There was no social life in Prairie, Texas. I worked the same schedule that I had back in Podunk with Wednesday afternoons and every Sunday off.

My routine every Wednesday was to buy a six-pack of beer and rent a VCR movie. On some Sundays, I would make the long drive back to Podunk to see Mama. Mama always had a big home-cooked meal waiting for me. She always sent me away with a big pot of pinto beans. I was paying my bills. It was a nice little life.

One evening as I was halfway through my movie and the beer, there came a knock on the door. It was Tara.

"Hi, Will, I was out jogging and thought I would drop by to see your place."

"Jogging? I didn't know you jogged. Come in. Would you like anything? All I have is beer and peanuts."

"Do you have any candy?" she asked.

"Uh, no, I don't keep candy."

"That's okay. I'll try a beer. I used to drink a little in high school with my girlfriends."

"Luckily, I still had three left. Tara quaffed the first one in just a few minutes."

"Wow! That was good. Do you have another?" she asked.

"Yes," I brought her the last one and she swallowed it almost as quickly as the first one.

"I can see that you're a natural beer drinker," I said. "You'd better slow it down, maybe just slowly sip the next one," I cautioned her.

"I'm getting dizzy-headed," she said. "Where is your bathroom?"

"It's next to the bedroom. I was just finishing my beer when Tara came out of the bathroom.

"Will, can you help me with this. I can't get my bra fastened."

I entered the bathroom. She was nude from the waist up. The biggest breasts I had ever seen were staring at me like headlights on the bright setting.

"Oh, never mind, you don't mind if I go shirtless for a little while do you? It's so hot outside."

I was taken aback. "Sure, no problem, get comfortable. We can finish the movie."

Within a minute, Tara was sitting on my lap. We began kissing and she didn't go home until the movie was over. I never knew how the movie ended.

The next day at the store, I was doing an ad for the weekly paper when she announced to her mom and dad,

"Will and I are going steady!"

"Oh, that's great!" exclaimed Rita, her mom. "I knew there was something special about little Will when he arrived that first day."

Her father piped in. "Now, boy, I know I work for you, but you need to be good to my little girl. If I thought you were two-timing her, I would throw you out the window."

Damn, I said to myself. *What have I gotten myself into? This has escalated quickly. I knew that I should have stopped things before they got complicated, but it was just easier to go with the flow.*

Time went on. For the next three years, we were an item with me being the reluctant party. Tara had begun staying with me close to half the time. One day I had a plan. I called Uncle Charlie.

"Hi, Uncle Charlie, this is Will."

"What's wrong? What is the problem?"

"Oh, no problem. I wanted to ask you something?"

"You need money. I need to warn you that…"

"No, Uncle Charlie. I don't need money."

"You don't have a problem and you don't need money? Well, that's just great. How is the family?"

"Everyone is fine. The store is doing well. That's what I wanted to call you about. I would like to put my name in the hat for a larger store. I want to grow with the company."

"Will, you have a good setup where you are. Besides, we can't find many managers that would move to Stonie, Texas, to take your place. But I'll look into it and see what turns up."

Great! I thought. For the second time, my way out of my problem was to move, and for the second time, the move would result in more money. My little life was turning around. It wouldn't be easy, however, telling Tara goodbye.

It was just a week after my conversation with Uncle Charlie that he called me back. "Will, how would you like to move to Jackson, Kansas. The manager, who's been there for over 20 years, wants to retire to spend more time with his ailing wife. Your salary would increase $400 a month and the bonus could be almost double what you make now."

I would have moved to Bumfuck, Egypt, for the same salary. This was the opportunity I'd been looking for.

"Uncle Charlie, I'll take it. I promise to do you a good job there. When can I move?"

"Hold your horses, Little Willie. We have to get you a replacement."

I've always hated the name Little Willie, but I wasn't going to say anything now.

"Okay, no problem, I'll be standing by. By the way, please don't tell any of our employees that I might be moving. You know how upset some women can get when they don't know who the next boss will be."

The wailing and gnashing of teeth was unbelievable when I told Tara that I would be leaving. It was a pandemonium that I never expected and wasn't ready for.

When I arrived at work the next day, the situation had escalated. The three of them met me at the freight door.

"I hope you're happy that you're breaking my little girl's heart," her mom told me.

Her father chipped in, "I don't think your Uncle Charlie will be too happy when he finds out that you've seduced a young employee of the company. I'm going to call him personally and tell him what a lout you are."

"Look, I haven't taken advantage of anyone. I was offered a promotion and I agreed to take it. Tara and I can still stay in touch. I'll come back to see her whenever I can." I lied.

"You should know that the three of us are thinking about quitting. How do you think that will look on your record when you open the doors and there are no workers except for yourself?"

The three of them had me over a barrel.

"Well, what do you want me to do? Stay here? Forever? In this shitty little town?"

"Do the right thing and marry the girl," her father said. You two are in love, aren't you?"

"Look, Tara can come with if she wants. I'm not promising anything. Nobody tells Will Perch who to marry."

I thought that it saved face for me and still made for a compromise. Maybe Tara wouldn't want to leave the security of a job and rent-free home for the opportunity of living with me when I was unsure about marriage.

My hopes were soon dashed.

"Will, that's what I've been waiting to hear. I'll go with you wherever you go. We can always be together." Tara was happy again.

I tried to force a smile. My plans were not working at all. Maybe I should have left like a thief in the night and let the chips fall. At least now there was peace, and we could move forward.

The time came all too soon to work out any other solution when Uncle Charlie called me the next day.

"Well, Willie, it's time to pack that bag and move on to the next big thing. You're going to like Kansas. You ready?"

"Yes, there is only a thing or two to do before I move."

"I thought your bags would have been packed weeks ago," Charlie said. "Are you having second thoughts?"

"Uncle Charlie, I need to tell you something. Tara wants to come with me."

"I won't get into your personal business, but don't let it affect your work."

Uncle Charlie was no help to counsel me. The time came, and this time, two of us traveled.

*   *   *   *   *

"Damn Will, it sure looks like the family was blackmailing you," declared Aunt Jinks. "How old were you at that time? You were too young to get married."

"You're absolutely right, Aunt Jinks. I look back at those days and ask myself about two things: one, how did I get married to women I didn't ever want to marry in the first place? I never wanted to marry either of my ex-wives."

"What is the other thing?" Aunt Jinks asked.

"Well, I don't know how that when I marry someone, they gain a hundred pounds. It happened to both the exes within the first two years that we were married."

I was serious, but Aunt Jinks couldn't stop laughing. "I don't know, but I'll help you find your next wife. We'll start out with an older woman, skin and bones. Maybe if the next one hasn't gotten fat by age 40, it won't be as likely," she joked.

By now, we were out of New Mexico and driving across the hot Arizona desert.

It was exciting to be embarking on a new phase of my life. A new beginning is just what I needed. I felt stagnant, staying in a rut I could not get out of. No money, no job, and a little pickup truck that couldn't be counted on. The new world for Will Perch was just around the corner. My little life would begin again.

"Did you and the young girl marry when you reached Kansas?" asked Aunt Jinks.

"Actually, no, Aunt Jinks. We married before we left Texas. I accepted my fate that I was going to end up with Tara. Besides, she was pregnant. That's another thing. We weren't sure at the time, but the signs were there.

"I have never been careful enough about using birth control. Both wives got pregnant pretty quickly, both accidentally, or that's what they told me.

"Tara's mother was relieved that Tara would be going with me but wasn't so sure if I would stay with her daughter without the influence of a marriage certificate. She and her husband decided quickly to remedy the situation.

"Tara's mom got it in her mind that a quickly planned wedding would be in order, just to tie up loose ends and keep us united. I didn't protest, now knowing that Tara might be in the family way. I had accepted my fate.

"I was slated to report to work in Kansas on a Monday, and on the previous Saturday night, we had tied the knot. We had decided to honeymoon after we saved up a little money first."

"Will, did Missy make it to your wedding?"

"No, I'm a little regretful that I didn't tell her until after the fact. It happened all so quickly. I called Otis. He was the only brother that had a car that would run. I asked him to drive down and stand in for me when I tied the knot.

"I remember calling Otis on the phone.

"Hey Otis, this is Will. I'm getting married tomorrow. Can you drive down to Stoney and stand in for me? I need a best man."

"Wow! Are you kidding me? I didn't know you were engaged."

"I wasn't," I said, "This has come about suddenly."

"Oh, a white shotgun wedding like in the old days!" my brother laughed. "My big brother got caught. Ha ha. Sure, I'll leave in the morning. Luckily, I just got paid. I can't ask off because I know they'll say no. I'll call in sick when I'm on the way."

Otis worked at the gas station. I felt that I would be blameworthy if he lost his job, but I hoped he would come to the wedding.

Otis was in his cowboy hat and boots. He made an incompatible match in the picture with the bride's maid, Tara's younger sister, Lulu, who seemed to be attracted to him.

"Are you a real cowboy?" Lulu asked.

"I've attended many a rodeo in my day," Otis replied. "I'd sure like to give you a ride on the bronco sometime." He winked.

The beer flowed and Otis' tongue became loose. I had never seen him like this. He could hold his liquor as well as my new bride, or so I thought at the time. He guzzled the red spiked punch, beer, and whiskey after a full meal of spaghetti. It was more than I could have handled.

"Where are you staying tonight?" Lulu's mother asked Otis.

"I'm planning on getting a room at the Motel 6."

"You'll do no such thing. Tara will be honeymooning with Will there, and you can stay in her room in our home. It was so nice of you to drive that long distance on short notice."

"Well, thanks, ma'am. I'll just take you up on it."

"Lulu, show Tara's room to Otis. I'll bet this little cowboy is ready for bed."

Lulu led Otis to Tara's room. She whispered, "Otis, I'd like to ride that bronco tonight."

"Sneak back in here after your folks go to bed. I'll show you how to ride. We'll have to keep the television on just in case you get excited with all the bucking," he winked again.

"I'll be back at 11:00 p.m."

"It was three in the morning when the long day caught up with Otis. Still in bed with Lulu, he began gagging and heaving, projectile vomiting spaghetti, meatballs, beer, and red punch from one end of the bed to the other."

"What in the hell is going on here?" Both parents' silhouettes darkened the doorway to the bedroom. "Oh my God! You get your skinny cowboy ass out of my house and never come back! Do you hear me, you little hillbilly?"

"Lulu did Otis take advantage of you," Hazel was screaming! "That little family is nothing but ghetto trailer trash!"

I was afraid that she might have a heart attack.

"No, Daddy, I fought him off. I thought I was being nice checking on him, and he tried to take advantage of me. But you'd be proud, Daddy. I was a good girl."

"This is the first time tonight, that you're telling the truth," Otis piped in. "You were a good girl all right. Good in bed!"

Hazel bitch-slapped Otis so hard that he keeled over backwards into his own vomit.

"Look at what you've done to my new bed linens! I just bought that new comforter and dust ruffle! You get out right now, or I'll call the sheriff and have you arrested!"

Otis took his jeans, boots, and hat in hand and hurried past Hazel while she got one last parting shot, a whack on the back of his head with a picture frame. Glass flew all over the floor.

"Damn, your family is crazy!" were Otis' last words spoken to my new in-laws on my wedding night. We heard all about it the next morning.

The deed was done, and life began anew. I was now a married man. In my early twenties, I had a high school degree, a car now paid for, and a wife with a baby on the way. Grown-up life had come upon me all too fast.

I had dreaded married life. I had never had the experience of being single and making money at the same time. It was something that I had always looked forward to. To this day, it hasn't happened yet.

I accepted my fate. Even with the sadness and regret of losing my single life to an early marriage, I was to find that I was to enjoy being married. Tara was a good housekeeper and was thrifty. She kept me in clean clothes and ironed my shirts. For the first time in my life, I had a little cash saved. She was a good money manager.

I was a young executive in a large respectable furniture store and the marriage and child made me appear stable and more mature.

The economy in Kansas was booming. Business was good. One day, I received a call from Uncle Charlie.

"Will, you're doing a great job in Kansas. It's nice to see how you've evolved and grown into the position of a professional manager. We're going to send you to market in Dallas with the buyers and a few other managers.

"You can help to make selections for your store. Have you ever flown?"

I couldn't believe my ears. I was going to fly in a plane and do corporate work, all at the company's expense. Mama and Maw Maw would sure be proud of me to hear about this.

Both my old high school buddies and my teachers would be so surprised to hear how well that young Will Perch was doing with his life.

I get scatterbrained when I am nervous. I could hardly sleep before taking that first plane ride. I didn't know the system or routine. It would have been nice if someone would have told me about navigating my way around the airport.

The morning came and Tara dropped me off at the airport. I had purchased a new cheap suit from the local Levine's boy's department. The suit had needed a lot of alterations, which I had left at the store to be done. I didn't try it on before my trip.

I put on the suit in the morning for the first time. Tara took me to the airport. I was as nervous as a whore in church. I watched people and followed some of them, while trying to figure out what to do and where to go. I didn't want to ask too many dumb questions to strangers and sound like an idiot.

I observed that many were looking at the big electronic board. The board displayed flight numbers and times. This is just the information that I needed.

I wrote down my gate number and was walking towards it when I felt an unfamiliar cool breeze.

I looked down. *Damn! my crotch is not sewn up! The bitch who did my alterations didn't finish sewing up the seat! My boxers were on display for the world to see!*

I set my briefcase on a bench and hurried into the men's bathroom to check the damage in private. It was bad.

"Dammit to hell! My briefcase!" I ran outside the bathroom only to find it gone. My money, my ticket, my notes were all in that briefcase, stolen in a matter of seconds!

Like a beggar, I began asking strangers for money. I got a few dollars and coins and found a pay phone. Luckily, I remembered Uncle Charlie's number.

"Hi, Uncle Charlie. This is Will. I'm at the airport."

"Hello, Will, are you excited about coming to market?"

"Well, I have a problem. Somebody stole my briefcase. The bastard got my travel money and plane ticket."

There was silence on the line. "How did that happen? How did they take it away from you?" he asked.

"Well, I didn't see them take it. I was in the bathroom."

"I don't understand, you didn't take your briefcase with all your valuables in it with you to the bathroom?" he asked.

"No, I accidentally left it on the bench outside the bathroom. I was flustered that the damned alteration lady didn't sew my pants up. My whole crotch is out, and my underwear is showing.

"When I remembered that I had left my briefcase outside, I ran outside the bathroom to get it, and some bastard had already stolen it."

"Have you checked the "Lost and Found"? Charlie asked.

"Lost and Found"? Where's that?

"Will, you'll have to ask around to find out. I'll call Tara to come back to the airport to get you. You can catch up with us on the next trip."

I was devastated. "When is the next trip?" I asked.

"We'll probably be coming back in six months. Bye." Uncle Charlie sounded angry and disappointed.

Damn it all! I had so looked forward to going to my first business meeting, with other managers. A chance to be recognized, all ruined because of an inept seamstress bitch.

I was sitting on the tall cement curb when Tara drove up and took me back home.

*   *   *   *   *

Aunt Jinks looked at me pensively. "Will, despite that shotgun wedding and shaky start, what happened between you and the young girl? From what you've said, she seems like she was making you a good wife."

"Looking back, Aunt Jinks, she was a good wife. She was bossy as I believe that most wives are, but I was doing well when I was with her. It was the first and really only time of my little life that I was getting ahead. We owned a small brick home and a Kawasaki motorcycle with 450 cc. Man, that bike would run.

"We each had a car. When my Datsun finished dying after 200,000 miles, Uncle Charlie let me drive an old company car. It drove well and best of all, it was free. The company paid for the insurance and I just had to buy gas.

"I guess you'd never think, seeing me now, that I was ever on top of things, and that my world was going right."

"Tell me, what happened? Did she find another boyfriend? It sounds like the old story."

"I'll tell you, Aunt Jinks. I just want you to know, it's not a pretty story."

I came home from work one day and we had a visitor.

Tara introduced us. "Will, this is Suzie. She's going to be staying with us for a while."

"What? That's nice," I said, "How long is a while?"

"I'm exploring my options right now," Suzie said. "My husband just left me for a floozie. I'm looking for a job and my own place. I wouldn't think it will be more than a few weeks."

"Oh... I see. Tara, would you get me an Advil and a beer? I'm getting a headache."

That night, I asked Tara, "What in the hell are you thinking? We have a child now and are just getting on our feet. Why did you invite an interloper to stay with us for such a long time? Can't we get her to move out sooner?"

"Suzie was my best friend in high school back in Stoney. She married a cowboy loser, like your brother Otis. She went home early one day, with take-out spaghetti for dinner, and caught him in bed with the school janitor's daughter."

"It seems that spaghetti is a bad omen in this family."

"Can you give her a job at the furniture store? She is a good salesman. She has a gift of gab that customers would love."

"I really don't want to start hiring people just because they're friends. They usually don't make good employees and it's hard to fire them, if I need to do so later."

"Just see what you can do. She has to have a job before she can get her own apartment."

There was no privacy with Suzie in the house. She left clothes all over the floor and wet towels. She was a slob. I was surprised that Tara let her get away with it when she wouldn't let me do it.

A week later, my best salesman quit me to work for the competition for a 10% straight commission. Tara overheard my phone conversation with Uncle Charlie.

"You've got to get a real go-getter to replace Freddie," he said. "That means interviewing a lot of people. Freddie's sales were double what any other salesman in the store had. You should not have let Freddie get away."

I didn't remind Uncle Charlie that I asked him about raising Freddie to 10% straight commission two months before he left us, and he had said absolutely not. Charlie didn't like to be reminded of anything he had done wrong.

"I have a person who has just applied who might make a replacement for Freddie," I said. "She has a gift of gab and is very persuasive."

"Well, then, get her hired. We have furniture to sell. The sooner the better."

I felt bad about working Suzie into the schedule when she obviously would never sell as much as Freddie sold. Freddie was a natural.

Maybe it would be a step that would result in getting her out of our house, although we would still have to deal with her at work. It was the first time that I put a personal concern ahead of my business. If we could first get her to move and then, later, if she could find a better job somewhere else, we would be shed of her.

Tara was pleased with me for giving her friend a job.

Suzie reported to work, but after a few paychecks, she still did not leave. By this time, we had gotten somewhat used to the living arrangement. With Suzie staying with us, on her days off, she watched over little Benny.

Tara began working part-time at the store, in the office, getting a break from baby boy. During these periods, when it was possible, Suzie babysat. It was an arrangement that worked for everyone, although I preferred our life as before, with just the three of us.

One day, as I am getting into the shower, there was Suzie, naked, stepping into the shower with me. I was astonished. "What in hell are you doing? Where is little Benny?"

Suzie was being playful. "You know what I am doing, little Mr. Handsome. Benny is taking a nap now, don't worry."

"I don't think this is a good idea." I said.

"I can see that you're beginning to think that it's a great idea. Now move over."

I tried to resist, but my natural instincts were stronger than my resolve.

We soaped and rinsed together, and of course, did much more. The whole act couldn't have taken over 20 minutes. We had just moved to the bedroom when we heard the door open.

In walked Tara, holding the baby. She had gone to work early but had forgotten her make-up bag and returned.

"You fat bitch!" Get out of my house. Is this how you repay your best friend? By screwing my husband, and ignoring my child?"

"Tara, it's not what it looks like," I stammered.

"Will, you get out too! You're just like your worthless brother Otis! I can't trust anybody anymore!"

We left the house hurriedly. I remember that Tara was holding the baby, both were crying.

We got into my company car and drove to work.

"Thanks to you, we're in real trouble now," I told Suzie.

"You're not completely innocent yourself," she said. "Don't worry. These things always blow over."

I held some comfort in her words, although I knew in my heart they weren't true. Shit would hit the fan over this. Things would not blow over.

I felt that I should have left Suzie at work and gone back home to explain my side of the situation, and smooth things over. I have looked back many times with regret that I didn't do that, but I was behind at work. Ads were due, and there were fires to put out. Once there, I could not get away.

Tara wouldn't answer my calls. She didn't come back to work either. I couldn't believe my bad luck.

At the end of the long day at work, I drove home. I had hoped that Tara had cooled off and come to her senses. I was ready to do my best to make things right.

I had a new plan now. I would kick the trespassing bitch out of the house and take Tara and little Benny on vacation. I wouldn't take no for an answer and I wasn't going to let Suzie stay another night.

My key would not open the door. Tara had the locks changed.

"Tara, what's going on?" I yelled. "This is my house. Open the door!" I was angry, and the neighbors began coming outside to see what was going on in this previously quiet neighborhood.

"Not anymore, it isn't. You gave it up when you started screwing my best friend. I can't believe you took advantage of her like you did."

"Took advantage?" I asked. I was just taking a shower getting ready for work when Suzie came into the shower with me. You can ask her."

"I don't need to ask her. She has already told me how you came into her bedroom and started taking advantage of her."

"That's a lie. She's twice my size. How do you think I would take advantage of her? She's a big fat hog, and a lying fat hog at that."

"Mama is coming tomorrow. We're going to figure out what to do. One thing is for sure, you cannot come near me nor the baby ever again."

And just like that, in one day, with no warning, my life began spiraling downward.

"What did you do?" Aunt Jinks asked. "It was your house, too. She had no right not allowing you inside your own house."

"I went to a hotel but couldn't get a room. Tara had our credit card and I never carried cash. I had to sleep in the car in my suit and go back to work the next day."

I called Uncle Charlie.

"Uncle Charlie, this is Will. I need to ask you for some advice.

"Sure, Will, ask anything. I'll help you if I can. By the way, how is that new saleslady working out for you?

"Not too well, but that is not what I wanted to talk about. This is more personal. Tara and I have had an argument and she's kicked me out of the house."

"That sounds serious. What did you do, Will?"

Why would Uncle Charlie automatically think the problem was my fault? "We had a guest staying with us. She is, or was, Tara's best friend from Stoney. I didn't even want her staying with us.

"To make a long story short, Tara caught her friend and me in bed together. It wasn't really my fault. Now I can't see my child or get into my house. What do you suggest that I do?"

"What is with you Perch boys that you're always screwing people you're not supposed to?" Uncle Charlie answered. "You'll have to make things right and get rid of your house guest."

"Uncle Charlie, the friend is gone, and it doesn't look like she'll be back. Tara won't let me come back in the house. Tara's mother is coming tomorrow and I'm afraid they'll want to sell my house out from under me. Can they do that? Can they take my motorcycle?"

"It doesn't look good, Will. I'll call Tara and try to speak on your behalf. You sure can get into some strange jams. Bye."

Luckily, the next day was payday, and I cashed the check and kept every penny of it. After two nights of sleeping in my car, I was ready for a shower and bed at the local hotel.

I really needed some different clothes. I drove by my house. "Tara," I yelled. "I need my clothes. I need the credit card, too. This is not fair that you're locking me out of my own house."

"Mama's here and we're going to the lawyer tomorrow morning. You're not coming in or ever seeing little Benny again."

"I'm not leaving until I have some clothes."

In a few minutes, she came to the door. "Your clothes are in two big black trash bags outside the back door. Now take them and git!"

I picked up the bags and drug them to my car. If she was getting a lawyer, then I knew this was serious, maybe beyond rectifying. I could go back to the hotel, but my cash would not hold out long at this rate.

"Will, I can't believe that she wouldn't take you back," said Aunt Jinks. "She was overweight and with a young child. Those are two factors against her finding another husband, I would think."

"She was blinded by her rage. She couldn't see anything except me being in bed next to Suzie. I tried my best to change her mind. Later I called Uncle Charlie."

Charlie was angry at me. He had told my mom and gotten her worried. I know poor Mama was disappointed. She had such high hopes for me. Gordon's second wife had left him and Mama was having to keep his daughter while he looked for a job.

Things weren't looking good for the Perch boys at that time. Young Freddie had dropped out of high school for no reason.

Mom called me at the store the next day.

"Will, What the hell is going on? You don't call your old mama anymore."

"Mama, I'm having a few problems, but nothing to worry about or that I can't get out of. I've just hit a little snag right now."

"Will, I don't care what you've done. You're my own flesh and blood and I'll stand by you." She was loyal to a fault.

"Do you need any money?" she asked.

The fact was my funds were low. I was living in a cheap hotel and trying to continue to manage a store.

"I might could use a little loan until I can get things straightened out."

Mama sent me $300.00 cash. I've never felt so low as to have to take that money from her. I knew her income was at poverty level.

Meanwhile, Suzie was still working at the store and selling furniture. She wasn't selling as much as Freddie did but wasn't doing badly.

She apologized for lying to Tara about our tryst.

"Tara has been my friend since junior high school. I couldn't tell her that what occurred was mostly my fault. I hope you understand. Besides, you two weren't meant for each other."

"Mostly your fault? It never would have happened if you hadn't come into the shower with me."

"Look" she said, "We've got to make the best of a bad situation. We're both living in fleabag hotels and struggling to get by. We work at the same place. Why don't we get a little apartment together? We can split costs and carpool."

Aunt Jinks, the world can be a crazy place, and events can occur in a moment, that you can never remedy or rectify. You only react.

My marriage was beyond repair. I knew that by this time. I was wanting peace, and to follow the path of least resistance, right or wrong. I was depressed all the time.

I took Suzie up on her proposal. I checked out of my hotel and moved my trash bags of clothes in with Suzie.

Suzie was fun, in a different kind of way. She was more free-spirited and fun-loving, two aspects missing from Tara's personality. Maybe that's why Tara was taken with her.

On the other hand, Suzie was lazy and a terrible housekeeper. We found that we got along together about as well as I did with Tara. She was no better with money than I was.

Meanwhile, Tara had filed for divorce, and filed for sole custody of our son, little Benny.

I called Uncle Charlie.

"Uncle Charlie, do you think I should fight the divorce, and get my own lawyer?"

"With what?" he answered. "You could incur a lot of debt fighting a losing cause. My advice to you is to give in to all her demands. Maybe when she sees that you are contrite, she'll let up on you. You may get redemption. Just give her everything she asks for. That is my advice."

"I don't know if that's a good idea. I don't see her letting up at all and half of the house, car, and other items are mine. I only want my half."

"You asked my advice and I've given it to you."

"Uncle Charlie, wait a minute! You said you would talk to her on my behalf. Did you call her? What did she say?"

"Will, I told her what I've told you. You were wrong in what you did, and I told her that I would discourage you from fighting her for the possessions. I told her that if you were generous in what she wanted out of the breakup, that hopefully, she would be fair, too."

"What was her response, Uncle Charlie? What did she say?"

"She said that she'd think about it."

"Aunt Jinks, it was the worst advice I ever followed. She mistook my generosity for guilt. She took everything. Now I wish I had gone down fighting. Uncle Charlie was successful and right most of the time, but he sure had it dead wrong on this issue. Tara would have sentenced me to death if she could have."

After 10 years of success in my new business, I was down to nothing, starting over from scratch.

Suzie and I moved into a little cheap apartment on the east side of town. We began to make a life. Things got better with time, though our lifestyle was never like it was with Tara.

Neither of us were organized or good with managing our own money. Our lives became a reflection of our personal habits: disheveled, unkept, and disorganized.

Uncle Charlie learned that Suzie had replaced Freddie at the store and that Suzie and I were living together. He became furious at me and never forgave me afterwards. If he and Mama had not been brother and sister, I'm sure I would have lost my job.

Otis called me one day. "Hey Bro! How's it hanging? Are you still shacking up with that huzzy?"

Although Otis behaved badly at my wedding, I still felt like I owed him for coming through for me on that wild day. It seems now that my first wedding day was cursed, and that Otis' episode was an omen for things to come.

I didn't appreciate his calling my "girlfriend" a huzzy, although it was hard to argue otherwise. I didn't correct him.

"Hi, Otis! Thanks for calling. It's so nice to hear a friendly voice for a change. You know all about my incident with Suzie. Yes, we're living together now."

"Will, by your living together, it makes you appear even more guilty with your incident with little Suzie. It doesn't matter to me. I've got no right to judge, and if I did, I wouldn't do so because we're brothers in the cause."

"The cause for what?" I asked.

"The cause for trying to get out of the trouble that we get into. How about I come up for a few days to drink a little beer and rehash Podunk days? Maybe we can smoke a few J's."

"Otis, that would be nice but we're struggling to get by in a little one-bedroom apartment. I've been knocked down to zero with this divorce I'm going through. Now the bitch wants child support, or she won't ever let me see my son."

"I thought Mama said that you couldn't see him anyway."

"That's true. That's why I'm not going to pay it. I tried to get back with her after the uh, incident, and she wouldn't have me. Now, I'm sure as hell not going to reward her for it.

"She can go to hell, the sooner the better!

"Anyway, you can't come now. We have no room, but thanks for calling."

"One more thing Will," Otis said. He became more serious. "Will, you are in a mess now, and may be for a long time because of that boy of yours. I'd sure hate to see you make the same mistake with the floozie you have right now."

"What do you mean, bro?"

"When these women want to latch their claws into you, they get pregnant. After that, the game is over. For you to have two sons, by two different wives, will cripple you for life."

"What the hell are you talking about?"

"I'm talking about birth control. You'd better be practicing it some way or another, or you'll find yourself in a real mess. You know that history can repeat itself."

Otis was never considered to be a bright boy or a deep thinker, but what he was saying sounded profound. The last thing I needed was for Suzie to get pregnant with my second child. I would be better off to shoot myself than to see that happen.

"Bye, Otis, thanks for calling."

Otis' message lingered in my mind for most of my waking hours for the next two weeks. I abstained from any kind of sexual pleasure.

As curses tend to do, this one presented itself at a most inopportune time.

After a long difficult day during our sidewalk sale, I came home and asked Suzie, "How about a cold beer? We've both had a pretty good day today with the big sale. Do you want to go out for Mexican food?"

"Here is your beer, but I won't be drinking one, she smiled. Guess why?"

I looked at her sneaking, deceitful, smiling face and became physically sick. In the back of my mind, I knew. She was in the family way. I never had time to plan. Otis' words came back to haunt me.

The realization made me depressed to a depth that I never thought possible. I should have heeded Otis' warning, or thought about the possibility myself, long before now.

When I recovered, I returned from the bathroom. "Suzie, Let's discuss this. Do you think we're ready for a baby? We're just getting on our feet for the first time. You know, we don't have to have this baby."

"It's too late to back out of fatherhood if that's what you're talking about. This baby is coming, like it or not. Our little bundle from heaven will be here in 7 months."

I could now see that Suzie was a little bigger. I had just thought that she was getting fat like Tara did. I don't know what it is about my girlfriends or wives, that after they're with me for a time, they become obese. It hasn't failed yet.

"Will, we need to get married, and give this boy a respectable name. Do you want to invite your brothers? Maybe Gordon would like to be a best man, or Freddie?"

"Hell no, I don't want brothers at my wedding anymore. It's bad luck. We'll just go to the justice of the peace or run off and elope."

So, there I was, slated for another wedding, in which I was the reluctant groom. Why was my life doing this to me? Why is Jesus punishing me?

Aunt Jinks brought me out of my story, which I was reliving. My heart was racing just while I was telling it.

"So, you married this floozie whom you didn't want to marry, history repeating itself."

"Yes, Aunt Jinks, except this time, I had no real way to back out of it since there was already a baby on the way: an 18-year commitment of child-care expenses, school, doctors, and eventually a car."

"So, what happened to this marriage?" Aunt Jinks asked. "Did the two of you get along well?"

"Yes, we did. We went through all the motions of expecting the baby, including child-birth classes. We moved to a larger apartment. My little life began again. If anything was consistent, it was that the Kansas economy was good and our store was riding the high wave."

It was just a couple of years later that I had a nice company car. The company had explicit instructions that only the store manager could drive the company car assigned to him.

I had however, allowed Suzie to, at times, drive my car against store policy. But we were far from the corporate office and who was to know?

Suzie was a big girl by this point and had begun going to the gym. She was twice my weight. One day she called, crying.

"Will, we're in trouble! I just wrecked the car!"

Oh, damn! I thought. *Her name will be on the police report. If this gets back to the corporate office, I'm in big trouble. I wish I had the backbone to tell her to drive her own damn car.*

I went out to the scene. Luckily, no one was hurt. It was drivable, although the windshield was out. When the police left, I drove it home with the cold Kansas wind blowing in my face.

There are times Aunt Jinks, when events in the world continue on without change for years, without some catalyst to change the routine of regimen. Life was moving along at a steady pace, until the morning of that wreck. My little life took a bad turn on that day, and I was forever changed.

On the way home, I noticed an envelope in the console. It was in Suzie's writing, and was covered with stars and hearts, like you might see in junior high. I assumed it was for little Nick, our child.

I was home now with the wrecked car parked in the alley behind our house when I took out the envelope and read it.

It was not a love letter for little Nick. It was not a love letter for me! It was a love letter for Shawn, the trainer at the gym. The fat bitch was screwing around on me.

I turned the windowless car around and drove straight to the gym.

I went into the weight room and saw the big guys working out. "Which one of you bastards have been screwing my wife?"

They looked at me incredulously, mouths agape. I referred to the note. "Which one of you bastards is Shawn? I am going to kick some ass!"

"Shawn is not here today. You might come back tomorrow at 1:00 p.m.," one of them answered.

I drove my wreck back home and I rushed into the house with the letter in hand. Suzie was getting ready for work.

"What is the meaning of this? Are you screwing Shawn from the gym?" I yelled.

"Don't get excited, it's not what you think," she said.

Where had I heard that line before? I thought.

"I have to get ready to go to work," she told me in a very blasé fashion. "We can discuss this later."

"You're not going anywhere until I find out if you're screwing Shawn!"

"I'm not screwing Shawn," she said. "I did, once or twice, maybe a few times, but it doesn't mean anything, and I'm not planning to see him again."

"After all I've done for you, and you repay me this way." I was livid at this point.

Suzie threw her hairbrush at me and hit me square in the forehead. Temporarily dazed, I recovered, and tackled her and we started wrestling. The fight was on. To my credit, I was hitting her with an open palm.

I grappled my way on top of her and her hands were pinned under my leg. I pulled her pants down and I began slapping her big fat ass with my hand. It turned as red as a radish.

Little Nick had watched the whole scene and was crying. "Don't hurt, Daddy!" he cried.

"Nicky, get on the phone and call 911! Call 911 right now!" Suzie cried.

"Don't do it, Nick!" I yelled loudly. "Mommy needs a spanking because she has been very bad! Don't touch that phone!"

"Nick called 911 and told the operator. "Daddy is giving Mommy a spanking. She's been bad."

I was not in my right mind when I released Suzie. We were both red and bruised and breathing hard.

"You're in trouble now. The police will take you away!" she screamed.

"You think I'm in trouble? Just watch this!" I went to the closet and pulled out Paw Paw's old 20-gauge shotgun. It was an empty weapon, but I wanted to get her attention.

"Who is in control now? You will do what I tell you. You will listen to me for the first time, you two-timing bitch."

"No, you will listen to me!" said a deep voice from the doorway. This is the police! Drop your weapon now and lie on the floor with your hands behind you!"

I dropped the shotgun. "It's not loaded," I told the police.

"I was just trying to get my wife's attention. We have the situation under control. You can leave now."

"We're leaving now. And you're coming with us." They handcuffed me.

"Don't you want to hear my side of the story," I asked.

"We can see your side of the story. You will spend the next few days in jail thinking about your side of the story."

"Aunt Jinks, they hauled me away from my own home in handcuffs, and took me to jail, for something that wasn't even my fault. My wife was screwing around on me. She wrecked my car, and got me in big trouble with my bosses, and they hauled ME away in handcuffs!"

"Life is not fair, Aunt Jinks. Some people are lucky, and some are not. There's no way to change a person's luck that's he's born with."

"How long did you stay in jail?" she asked. "Did you get to tell your side of the story?"

"Aunt Jinks, I was in jail for two weeks. I saw the judge and explained my side of the story. He seemed to be sympathetic, but when I finished, he said,

"Will, you need to cool off. I'm sentencing you to two weeks in jail and you will stand trial for domestic abuse."

I called Mama. I was at an all-time low.

"Mama, I'm in jail. Can you call Uncle Charlie to bail me out? That bitch, Suzie, has been screwing around on me. Tell Uncle Charlie I'll be at the store the first thing in the morning."

Poor Mama didn't have funds to bail me out. She called Uncle Charlie. Uncle Charlie told her he would take care of it.

The next day, I was called out of my cell to receive a phone call.

"Will, this is Uncle Charlie. I see you've gotten yourself in a big mess now."

"Uncle Charlie, I can explain. If you can bail me out, I'll explain what happened. I'll call you from work."

"Will, there's no hurry along that line," he said.

"In fact, Will, there is no more work. We've got somebody lined up to come up and run the store. You're on your own now. I've done for you what I could. You're not cut out for the furniture business."

"This little time in jail just might be what you need."

"Uncle Charlie, don't you want to hear my side of the story? The fat bitch was screwing around on me while I was at work."

"Oh, you mean she was doing the very same thing to you that you were doing to your first wife? Will, I've washed my hands with you. You're a hopeless loser. We're done."

Uncle Charlie fired me on the phone, in jail.

So, there I sat in my little cell alongside the crooks and criminals.

"Will, you poor little devil, that sounds cruel. Your Uncle Charlie, with all that money he has, could have helped you get out of jail and start putting the unpleasant past behind you. I swear, you Perch boys have all the bad luck."

"It sure seems like I've had more than my share of it," I replied.

"I predict your life will get better in Arizona. I left Texas many years ago and never looked back. It was the best thing my sister and I ever did. We love Arizona."

"What did you do when you finally got out of jail?"

"Aunt Jinks, I had no job waiting for me. Nobody wanted to see me, especially with my being unemployed. In that regard, I felt free. I missed the regular income but was actually pleased to no longer be working in the shitty retail business.

"What I had not realized is how much I missed little Nick. I would have considered going back to the two-timing bitch just to be with him as he grew into adulthood. It was not meant to be.

"Being denied contact with my first son, Benny, I was crestfallen to think I had two young sons and would never see them or have anything to do with either of them while they were growing up."

I collected my clothes and whatever things that Suzie didn't want from our apartment. Otis took me back to Podunk to stay with Mama for a while to sort out my future.

Otis had problems in his past finding work and ended up back in the grocery store where I used to work. He was doing well and learning to cut meat with my old pot-head friend Paolo.

If there was any luck on our part, it was from the death of my grandfather on the farm. He had been a successful farmer.

He left Mama enough money to get out of debt and buy an old, but larger and more comfortable home in Podunk. The home that we grew up in eventually became condemned when the roof caved in.

It was the only time in Mama's life that she ever had any money. She used a portion of it to buy me a small pickup truck and a lawn mower. At 35 years of age, my profession was to begin: mowing people's lawns. I began my new career.

"I wasn't proud of my work, but it brought in cash, all tax free. I got paid almost as soon as I finished the jobs. I was outdoors all the time and for the second time in my little life, I was getting ahead. And, for the first time in my life, I was not shackled by a conniving wife whom I didn't want to be married to."

"Business was great in the summer months, but the work was seasonal, and in winter, there was little or no income. I was more the grasshopper than the proverbial ant.

I spent the money when I made it and struggled during the winter months. I searched for a job that paid a regular weekly paycheck. My background was in retail, so I answered an ad I saw in a window."

If a person can't find a job anywhere else, he can always find one in a fast-food restaurant. I donned my Levine's suit and Mabel's tie, still with the smudge on it, and set up an appointment.

The chain I interviewed was Sam's Chicken and Biscuits. I think it used to be called Sambo's Chicken but had to change the name because of the racial climate going on at the time.

I couldn't believe my good luck as I landed a salaried position as a traveling district manager. I moved to Louisiana and rented an apartment. I could hold my head high again. My salary was more than what tightwad Uncle Charlie had been paying me to manage the furniture store.

My job duty was to travel my route of stores, and review schedules, check sales, deposits, and help out with general problems. I even attended chicken and biscuit school in Baton Rouge and learned how to fry and to bake. I received a diploma.

I wanted to succeed for me, my mom, and to show Uncle Charlie that he had made a big mistake by giving up on me. He explained his actions to Mama, but I know that in her heart, she never forgave him for abandoning me in jail.

"Where was your second wife at this time?" Aunt Jinks asked. "Did you two get a divorce? Was she coming after you for child support?"

"She might have. I don't know. I do know that there was nothing to go after at the time as I was as broke as a joke. She knew that.

I called her one time while I was doing lawns, and we visited a while. She said she was filing for divorce, but in the meantime, I had to pay child support.

"Until our divorce is final, we're officially still married," I replied. "You can't sue your husband for child support. You don't know what the hell you're talking about." At the time I said this, I didn't know that she could come after me for it.

"Look," I explained, "When I can get ahead again, I'll send money, meanwhile, leave me the hell alone."

Suzie was screaming at this point. "I'm going to finish getting this divorce and come after you for both child support and what little savings you have."

"Okay bitch, do it. Don't talk about it. Just do it. I've got nothing to lose. Beware of the man with nothing to lose!"

"I'm sure the judge will be pleased to hear all about your boyfriend at the gym. I've kept that letter all this time just in case you stoop low enough to come after me. Keep that in mind, Fatso, and leave me alone!"

I didn't talk to Suzie for years after that conversation. Somehow, she made her way with the child in tow. Maybe she hooked up with the trainer at the gym. I don't know, and I don't care.

At work, I found myself going to my stores at four in the morning and baking biscuits, and later, frying chicken. It wasn't my job, but often the cooks didn't show up for work.

Our sales were good and my numbers were strong on the balance sheet, but I grew tired of it quickly.

"When I quit, I couldn't even smell a Sam's biscuit without gagging. It was time to move on again. I moved back to Podunk and began mowing lawns again. That brings us up to present. That is what I was doing when you came to visit."

Chapter 3
A New Life in Arizona

We arrived in Phoenix and I stayed in the little spare bedroom in her home. The next day I walked to a nearby supermarket. I went in and asked for a job.

Upon leaving, I espied a group of Mexican men. They appeared to be bullying a young woman. I told them, "Hey boys! Leave her alone!"

They turned and looked at me incredulously. The leader seemed to laugh, which caused all of them to laugh.

"Pendejo! Hey amigos, we have a miniature John Wayne here." They left the girl and surrounded me.

"What are you going to do about it? Do you know this senora?"

"No, but I do know that only cowards would beat up a woman."

The fight was on. I inflicted a few blows in the beginning but was no match for the three of them. I took hits and kicks from 3 different directions.

I had heard once to never go down on the ground if getting beat up. Most of the damage to a man is done by kicking and stomping him while he is down.

When they thought they had done enough damage, they left and took the girl with them. My clothes were torn, I had two black eyes, a broken tooth, and bruises and whelps on my legs and back.

"What in the hell happened to you?" asked Aunt Jinks. "I swear, you can get into more messes than anyone I know."

I explained. "I was trying to save a Mexican woman from getting beat up. This is my reward for it."

"Will, life is not like the movies. Good guys don't always win. The best lesson is to stay out of trouble. You Perch boys were never taught that."

The broken tooth affected my smile, so I had to practice doing so without showing my teeth. I was in no financial condition to go to a dentist.

Within two weeks, the human resources lady at the superstore called me. Most of my facial bruises were gone by then.

"Will, you have a lot of experience in grocery management. Can you come in for an interview?"

I had enhanced my history of duties at the store back in Podunk, hoping they would not do a background check.

In a week, I was working, and in two more weeks, I had my first paycheck in a long time. I spent the whole paycheck on groceries for Aunt Jinks.

"Thanks, Will, this is generous of you. Now that you're working, don't you think it's time that you found your own place to live? You can stay here as long as you want, but a man your age would want his own bachelor pad."

"Sure, you're right. I'll just stay only as long as it takes me to find my own apartment."

I found a nice apartment walking distance from Aunt Jinks' home and my work. I was longing for my wheels. I called Otis back in Texas.

"Hey Otis, how're you doing?"

"Just great, man. I've been promoted to assistant meat cutter in the butcher shop of the grocery store. I got a raise and things are really good now. I have almost a thousand dollars saved up. Oh, by the way, Lee asked about you.

"Otis, that's great. I need my little pickup truck. Could you help me to get it? I need to find my own digs and wheels to get to work and back. I'm 36 years year old. I can't live with Aunt Jinks forever. And incidentally, tell Lee to kiss my ass."

"Will, your piece of crap pickup truck wouldn't make it to Phoenix. It won't even start now."

"Otis, I hate to ask you this, but you've already told me that you had a thousand dollars. Could you get repairs done to whatever is wrong with the pickup truck and drive it out here to Phoenix. I'd be forever grateful and owe you a big favor anytime you would want to ask for it. I'll also pay you back with interest."

"I don't know," Otis said, "I hate to part with the most money I've ever had at one time. I'll think on it and get back with you."

"I'll think on it and get back to you" has always been a polite way of saying no. Otis has come through for me on more than one occasion, but this time, what I asked him to do, just might have been beyond his level of generosity.

Meanwhile, I walked to work.

My job at the superstore was going well. I was a favorite of the assistant manager. Both the general manager and the assistant manager worked salaried schedules, which meant that they were in the store at least 70 hours every week. The good part of their jobs was that they were compensated very well for it.

"Will, our company spans the western states. We are always looking for managers. I can see that you have manager capabilities. How would you like for me to put your name in for contention for a store in Colorado? It is smaller, but if you get the position, you'll never have to worry about money again."

"Thanks, Mr. Banks. I don't know if I want to move to Colorado. It's cold there and far from family. I'd rather move to Texas. Is there anything there available?"

"No, Will, there is no opening in Texas. I can't stress the importance enough of applying for this position. This is a rare opportunity. I would apply for it myself, except that I'm on track to get a different store of my own."

"Once you get the store running like it should, you'll have more opportunity to choose to manage other locations."

I should have listened to Mr. Banks. It was another fork in the road of life and I had chosen badly. He left soon afterwards for a top position in Utah. He told me he was leaving and that his replacement might be someone who would not appreciate my work. His replacement was Mr. Burns.

Mr. Banks and Mr. Burns could not have been more opposite. While Mr. Banks was encouraging and fun to work for, Mr. Burns was a tyrant.

"Hey Shortie, You'll need to work the graveyard shift next week." Mr. Burns said.

"Mr. Burns, I don't appreciate the nicknames. From now on, my name to you is Mr. Perch."

"Will, you're white, and you're male. That means you are not protected in any way from any minority rights group. So, Shorty, do as I say."

It was all I could do to keep from giving Mr. Burns a knuckle sandwich, but I needed the job and he knew it. He gave me the worst shifts and wrote me up for the tiniest infraction.

One day, he introduced a young black man who would be working in my department. His name was Du-wane.

Du-wane was lazy and sullen. Because Mr. Burns treated me badly, Du-wane became insubordinate. The days went by badly. I was having to do Du-wane's work when he would not do it.

After a few weeks, I had enough. I went over Mr. Burns' head and asked the general manager if he would move Du-wane to a different department and get me someone easier to work with.

The next day, I was introduced to Randy. As I was showing Randy around, we approached Du-wane.

Du-wane was sitting idly on an end-cap.

"Hi Du-wane, I would like to make introductions."

Du-wane said, "Nice to meet you, Randy. I hope you don't mind working for Mr. Burn's bitch, Will. I sho' don't like working for him."

"Don't mind what Du-wane is saying," I said. "He is smarter than he looks, and he talks trash, which is all nonsense."

Randy chuckled, and I continued on with the initiation and training.

The next day, Mr. Burns called me into his office.

"Will, are you a racist?"

"No, Mr. Burns, are you a racist in addition to being a sadist and a bully?"

"Will, I will conduct this interview. You need to know that I'm writing you up for making racial statements to Du-wane and insulting his intelligence."

"While you're at it, you need to put in another entry."

"I'll be glad to, what other item would you like on your report."

I jumped on Mr. Burn's desk and with one hand held his hair, which was a toupee that came off into my hand. With the other hand, I hit him square in the nose. I heard the pop and knew it was broken. Blood spurted across the room. I stuffed the toupee in my pocket.

"Put that in your report! Write me up for breaking my supervisor's nose, you ugly-ass bald-headed bastard!"

I knew better than to stay in the store any longer. I had burned yet another employment bridge. I was jobless again. I wasn't waiting around for police to show up and take me away.

As I drove home, I realized that I had never felt so good about anything in many years. Mr. Burns would never forget how he bullied someone just one too many times. Beware the fury of a patient man. I had read that somewhere. It sure was true in my case.

I was called back by the store for a corrective interview. In my estimation, they just wanted me to sign a resignation form and some document saying I wouldn't sue them. I didn't feel that returning to the store would aid me in any way.

"Sorry, but I won't come in. You might tell Mr. Burns to try to be easier on his next patsy and give up bullying. Bullying can have negative results, as he has learned. If he wants his wig back, tell him to come get it. It's in my home."

I never won ribbons, medals, or trophies. The only items among my keepsakes are my high-school degree, my diploma from Sam's Chicken, and the toupee.

Fifty years of age is the time of life when a man reaches his prime in his earnings. I found myself unemployed and burned out.

I have never sent money to either of my ex-wives or sons. There has never been any to spare. I hear that both boys are in college and have a future much brighter than I had at their age. I miss them more than they would ever know. Neither will have anything to do with me.

Times were actually getting better. I had decided that flipping burgers would be better than working for the public and the big box stores. There was one business that I knew, and I knew it well, and that was the yard business.

If you can find yards to mow in Phoenix, Arizona, you can mow them every week of the year. As long as the sod gets water, the grass will always grow.

The many years of the Mexicans sneaking across Mexico has taken a toll on the white American blue-collar worker. A Mexican will work longer and harder than a white man and will gladly do so for less money.

It was hard to get started in the business. Until I was working as much as I wanted, I had printed business cards to be distributed in good neighborhoods, with a hand-written note on the back, with the price I would charge for mowing, trimming, and blowing.

The first estimates were ridiculously low, as it was hard to undercut the going rates and get homeowners to switch yard men. With time, as I would secure more yards, I would raise costs to a profitable level. With each increase, I would lose a few yards, but I kept many good ones.

After a few months, I had more work than I could handle. The money flowed in every month of the year. By this time, I had a nice apartment with a large garage and a storage building.

Otis had gotten my pickup repaired and brought Mama out. Both were impressed with my lifestyle.

"Do you ever hear from my grandsons, little Benny and Nicky?" Mama asked.

"No, Mama, my fat ex-wives have poisoned them to me. She tells them what she wants them to hear, and there is no one to give them the truth. Life is not always fair, is it Mama?"

"Will, I have been on the other side and I can tell you that it's not easy being a single mother, raising children by herself. No Will, life is not fair."

"Well, it's more fair for some than for others. How is shit-ass Uncle Charlie doing? Is he still rolling in the dough? Still an executive with Slugs Furniture?"

"Yes, he's still there. He asks about you every once in a while. He said that you had potential for being a good store manager if you could have just stayed away from the women. You might have moved up in the company."

"Mama, with all the misfortunes I've had, I wouldn't go back to the furniture business if they make me vice-president, president maybe, but not even vice president. Then, if I were president, I would fire Charlie."

"How long do you think you'll be mowing lawns? It's a hard life isn't it?"

"I like working outside in the heat. It keeps me young and fit. I don't have an ounce of fat on me, even on my beer diet. The best of it all, Mama, is that I'm my own boss. There is no Uncle Charlie or Mr. Burns to push me around anymore. Life is good enough. Sometimes, enough is all you need."

"I just hate to see you work your youth away when there are easier jobs. You know, you could have stayed with the big Superstore. You didn't have to break your boss's nose."

"I guess you're right, Mama. I'll just work a few more years and get an inside job. These big stores are always looking for a hard worker."

Mama was crying, but she broke into a smile upon hearing my little white lie. Sometimes, lying is okay, if the greater good is done. Maybe she knew I was lying, and that she felt that I had at least been listening. Maybe she believed what she wanted to believe.

At that moment, I wanted to do something big, or nice, for her. "Mama, I'm going to buy you a new pickup truck, not the little Ford Ranger, but a full-size truck with all the bells and whistles, a big Ford F150."

"What I'd like is a white Toyota truck. Every truck you see on TV is a white Toyota. That's what I want." Mama was cheering up.

"Mama, I'm promising you now, I'll get that truck for you someday."

At the time I said it, I truly meant it with all my being. It wasn't until Otis began driving Mama back home that I realized the impossibility of my boast.

I'm not doing badly, but I never dared to dream of driving a Toyota myself.

I enjoyed my mom and brother's visit. I realized that I missed family and having some connections. What I didn't realize at the time was what the impact had on my younger brother. Otis called me within a week of returning to Podunk.

"Hey, bro. I'm coming back out to see you."

"You're welcome to come back, but why, when you've just seen me?"

"You ugly coot, it's not just you that is the reason for me to come back to Arizona. I'm just like you. I felt a sense of belonging in the big city. I've just tendered my notice to quit my job at the supermarket. I'm going to be moving in with you."

"Damn, Otis, I don't think that's a good idea. You've got a steady job that pays well for living there. It costs more to live out here than it does living back in Podunk. You can't get cheaper than Podunk."

"That's just it. With my experience, I know I'll get a job in a Piggly Wiggly or some other really big supermarket. I've heard that meat cutters in the big cities make double what I make. Besides, I saw that your nice apartment has two big bedrooms. So, as I see it, my expenses would be lower.

"Don't worry, I'll pay half of everything: utilities, groceries, and rent. Now how would you like to live on half of what it's costing you now, and have some excellent company besides?"

I couldn't say no to Otis. His life has not been easy either. He's helped me through rough times and stood up for me at my first wedding. The thought of cutting my expenses to one-half was intriguing also. Maybe I could save and buy Mama that white pickup after all.

"Okay, that's a great idea. When do you want to come?"

"I'll have to rent a little U-Haul trailer. I have lots of things now. I have begun collecting."

"What do you mean collecting? I don't want you to junk up my apartment or my garage. I need space for my yard equipment. You have to lock everything up every night here. The few times I have forgotten, some Mexican has stolen something every time. Last week, I lost a shovel.

"I have a nice collection of coke bottles, arrowheads, and old Playboy magazines. I have all of the Star Trek books.

"Will, how do you know they were Mexicans who stole it? Did you see them?"

"Otis, Mexicans are the only group who would steal a shovel to use it. You have to give this to them. They're hard workers."

"Will, I guess you're right.

"I don't have that much stuff, I'll give some of it to Mama, to watch over it for me. I'll be there in one week, just after my last payday."

"Well, come on if you're coming. See you then."

Otis pulled up in my old little pick-up truck. He had put in a new battery, radiator, hoses, and whatever else that was wrong with it when I had it. He had a hitch installed and was pulling a small U-Haul trailer.
"Well, Otis, I know you said it, but I didn't believe you. You're a sore sight for eyes.

"You mean a sight for sore eyes," he corrected me.

"Yes, you're right, it was a Freudian slip. I'm surprised that you didn't burn up a transmission in that little truck pulling that trailer."

"I had to go slow. I stopped in Ruidoso, New Mexico and spent the night sleeping in the truck. It's not very comfortable because the seat doesn't lean back. I almost froze to death."

I can't believe it can be 100 degrees in Roswell and just two hours away, a man can freeze to death at night. I didn't want to waste money on a high dollar hotel."

"The truck doesn't sound too good right now. I'm kind of surprised myself that I made it here with it. With the good times to come, I should be replacing it with a new one in no time."

"Well, it's good to be positive, but let's not get ahead of ourselves. Want a drink? I've just got beer."

"I don't drink much beer anymore. Ever since my last D.U.I., I've tried to quit. Nope, no beer, but I've brought you a special treat. My only vice, if you want to call it that, is occasionally imbibing in the smoking of the wacky weed."

"Weed and primo! Not the stalky shit you used to smoke with Paolo. I always say, 'Give me primo, or give me death!'"

"And I'm not just talking about weed. I'm talking about the women also. Will, you are a handsome man. You didn't have to settle for the fat, ugly ones. You could have held out for a pretty one."

"That's all past now, and if you're dead set on smoking primo every night, you can forget about getting ahead of life out here. I can't afford it myself."

Otis unloaded his car and trailer. Inside the trailer he had packed some shelf units, so his stuff (collections) fit pretty efficiently in the shed.

Chapter 4
Manuel and Antonio

I drove downtown where the unemployed immigrants hang out to try to get daywork. "Hop in," I said to a little man who did not speak English. "Trabajo para dinero. Work for money."

He reluctantly got into the truck with me. He was no larger than I was. I was to find that his name was Manuel, and that he was from Guatemala.

I paid him $10.00 hourly, which was a generous going rate at the time. I found that he worked even better than brother Otis. We had a day's work of yards done by noon. In Phoenix, that is ideal.

I began canvassing for more work. We made a good team. He taught me a little Spanish, and I taught him some English.

A few months went by and I found that I was pocketing more money by using him than I ever did when I worked alone. For the first time in my little life, I was an employer.

He was good with his money, better than I was. He lived in a nice apartment. But where I had only one roommate, he was living with 5 other men.

I found him to be honest, also. I sometimes worked until noon and let him finish the rest of the day of work by himself.

That situation set up the beginning of my friendship with Hugh Farnsworth.

Chapter 5
Hugh Farnsworth

I stopped at the Ritz Hotel, a fancy resort hotel with a bar, on Regal Street to get paid for having mowed the premises. After receiving cash, I stopped in the bar inside for a cold beer. There was a tall well-dressed man with a big mustache drinking at the bar with his arm around a local barfly. I sat back and watched him work from my table in the corner.

By and by, hand in hand, Hugh led the barfly to the elevator and up to his room. Thirty minutes later, he came back to the bar, red-faced, and with his hair now tousled.

"How much did you have to pay for your little girlfriend?" I asked. "I've been watching you and can see that you are a smooth operator."

He could have become angry at my statement and to know I had been spying on him, but I felt that he wouldn't want to get his hair messed up any more than it already was by trying to teach me some manners.

To my surprise, he was friendly. "It's the strangest thing," he said. "I was just nice to her. It cost me a few drinks, and some time flirting. The drink tab is on my company as I have a generous expense account, so it didn't cost me anything out of my own pocket."

"Sounds like a perfect setup to me," I replied. "If your drinks are free, then why don't you buy the next round for us?"

Hugh and I drank and visited outside beside the pool for the next few hours, exchanging our stories about life, women, hunting, and sex.

He worked for a large banking company that sent him out on Monday's and back home on Thursdays or Fridays, to sell equipment and software for their back offices.

He said that he was married and had a daughter, and that nothing would ever get in the way of his family.

"It seems to me that you're taking a big chance, doing just that, by chasing tail in a hotel." I said.

"There's no excitement in life without some risk and danger. Risk gets the mind working and the blood pumping. Often, I take clients out on the town. Usually, they want to go home early, and I go back out on my own to hunt.

"Sometimes, I take them with me. I can tell you two things. One, it helps sales. And two, it's a hell of a lot of fun. Otherwise, I would be in a hotel room alone, staring at four walls.

"You know, Will Perch, I had an uncle that I admired greatly. He always drove a fancy car and lived a charmed life. He told me. 'Hugh, when you're on that rocking chair, on your front porch, towards the end of your life, you'll look back and regret the things you didn't do, more than the things that you did do.'

"He encouraged me to have as much fun as I could while I could do it because life is short. I've heeded his advice ever since.

"If I were a single guy like you, I would be out all the time. A little cute guy like you would be surprised how many women you could get to know, in the Biblical sense, in a year's time."

"Hugh, I don't have a job, and I don't have an expense account," I said. "I'm just trying to keep my head above the water running my own little lawn business. Lately, the business has been very good. I'm not going to tempt fate now."

"Have you been to Mexico," Hugh asked me. "It's not that far away. I've gone online and met a woman or two at the border. They were so attractive that they could have been models.

"I brought some of them back to the USA and for a night or two of good times. It's easy, and they're easier to please, and with less money, and fewer drinks than these spoiled entitled American women."

"No Hugh," I said, "I have not tried that."

"It's something you should check into. You know, we're not getting any younger."

He left me with that thought and paid for my drinks.

After that afternoon, we met every month at the same bar, for an afternoon of visiting and comparing notes on how the most recent month had transpired for us.

I returned home and my equipment was already cleaned and put away in my shed. Little Manuel finished our work and went home. I felt guilty about letting him work while I drank in a nice, air-cooled bar in the best part of the town.

Sometimes, life just doesn't make sense. A few weeks after I met Hugh, Manuel informed me that he had a friend to arrive from Guatemala who was a good worker. Manuel was urging me to hire Antonio to work with us.

I picked up the two men, putting Manuel in charge. I had to give Manuel a two dollar per hour raise, because he was second in command of my little company. I took the two men to the worksite at the beginning of the week. And stayed with them while they mowed yards all day.

They did excellent work and were happy with their lot. I found myself not having to do the hard, physical work any longer. I was still earning enough money for my simple lifestyle, and in fact, saving because of Otis paying his share of his expenses.

I was the boss benefitting from underlings doing the work for me. I had been on the other side of this arrangement all my life. It felt good, but somewhat unjust. The Guatemalans were happy, so I continued on with the same arrangement.

Life seemed strange to me.

"How do you meet these women from Mexico?" I asked Hugh at our next meeting.

"Some of them in bars, and some online."

"Online, like a chatroom, on the computer?"

"No, on a singles site. Of course, I don't give out my real name. You could do it though, although I wouldn't advise it. Sometimes, the encounters don't go well and you don't want them to know where to find you."

"I don't have a computer."

"You need a computer and internet service. You could use the library's computer for free, but it would be better for you to work from your home or coffee shop, using your own laptop. Eventually, your love nest will span the world. Sometimes I search for someone in the next city that I'm going to visit in my work."

The next day I went into Computer World and bought a small laptop. I took it to the library to see if the girls working there could help me to navigate the system. I spent most of my spare time learning what I could. For several weeks, all I could do was turn it on and off and look up world maps.

Finally, I joined "I'mnotmarried.com" and began searching online for my first online date. I posted a picture and within a week, I was contacted by Deena, an Asian American from San Francisco.

Chapter 6
Deena

Deena worked for a web services provider in San Francisco. Her background could not have been more different from mine. We seemed to have nothing in common, but when she contacted me, we spoke on the phone and agreed to meet in a public place.

I waited in the Starbucks Coffee Shop and was about to give up on her when she walked through the door carrying a briefcase and pulling a small, wheeled, carry-on luggage cart.

She was wearing expensive clothes and sunglasses and looked very chic. She would learn quickly that I was a simple working man.

"Hi, Handsome. You're shorter than your photo shows. Do you always lie on your computer profile?" she asked.

"I didn't lie and I can tell already that you and I are not meant to be. Bye, bitch! I got up to leave."

"Hey, don't be so sensitive. We've gotten off to a bad start. Let's start all over. I'm Deena and I'm glad to have finally met you. Stay for a latté and I'll pay for it."

We visited for an hour or so. The conversation went easily but it seemed that we had absolutely nothing in common.

"Well, It's time for me to go? Are you staying in Phoenix on business? I see that you're packed."

"No, Will, I have my luggage and briefcase because I'm staying with you for a few days. You don't mind, do you?"

I couldn't believe what I was hearing. "Aren't you being a little presumptuous? We've just met and frankly, we don't have a lot in common. Are you playing me? Because I can tell you, you won't find money here. What you see is what get."

"Will, I'm a pretty good judge of character and I feel confident and safe staying with you for a few days. I want to see how you live, and what you do. It would be a true test of how we would get along. Incidentally, I certainly don't need your money."

"Deena, I have a small apartment with two bedrooms. My brother Otis is living with me. I'm not sure I could ask him to give up his bed and sleep on the couch."

"Will, that will not be a problem."

I looked her in the eye and knew that she had planned to sleep with me before she left California.

"Well, come with me and I'll show you the life of a poor displaced Texas boy."

In the apartment, she looked around and asked. "Will, do you have anything to drink? Like red wine?"

"No, I just have beer."

I opened a couple of cold ones. Before she had finished her bottle, she was kissing me. "Let's see where we'll be sleeping," she said.

I was thinking, *this doesn't seem real. If this is how computer dating works, I can see why Hugh was so keen on it.* We entered the bedroom, not to exit for a couple of hours.

I was worn out.

"Let's get something to eat," she said. "You've got to keep your strength up. We're just getting started."

Just getting started? I wondered.

She drove me to a fancy restaurant nearby that I had never been in before, in her rental car. It was a restaurant that I had seen many times driving by, but never entertained the thought to eat there. It exceeded my pay scale. We wined and dined and were back at the apartment for round two.

By the time the weekend was over, I was done for. She returned to her home and work. After her return to her 'city by the bay,' she called every day.

I did not answer the phone. I struggled through the week, continuing my yardwork, and never quite catching up on my rest. By Saturday night, I was winding down with a beer and hot dog when I heard a knock on the door.

I smelled her perfume before I saw her.

"Hi, Lover Boy! I hope you're rested up for a weekend of a good time. I was able to get a late flight to Phoenix and caught a taxi to get here."

The weekend went by as did the previous weekend, with the two of us coming up for air, and only every few hours for sustenance. I finally told her. "Deena, you have to go home. I can't keep up this pace. I need to rest up just to go to work."

"Are you running me off after all I've done for you? You are not a man; you are a mouse."

With that, she packed her things and went outside. "Don't worry about me," she said, "I'll find my own way back to the airport."

The next day I went outside, looking forward to a productive day with Manuel and Antonio. My truck was gone! My heart sank to my stomach when the thought came to me that somehow Deena was behind the theft.

It was difficult making the phone call when she had called me so many times and I did not answer.

"Hello Deena, how are you doing?"

"Better than you are you little ugly shit." She was still angry at me.

"I've had a stroke of bad luck. Somebody stole my pickup truck."

"Oh, is that right?" she asked. "Have you tried the airport? Sometimes people loan their vehicles to friends to go to the airport to catch their flights."

"Did you steal my truck and take it to the airport?" I asked. "You know I could go to the police and turn you in."

"You silly little hillbilly. It's not stealing when you give someone the key."

"I didn't give you the key." I replied.

"You have your story, and I have mine. What do you think that the police would say? I say that you gave me the key."

I had a chill go down my back when I thought back to giving my story to the police when they had hauled me in for spanking Tara.

"How did you get it? Look, never mind, I won't turn you in. Just tell me which terminal, and I'll find a way to get out there and retrieve it."

"You're a big boy now, and too independent to need my help. You're lucky I told you the general area. If you check all of the terminals, you could probably find it in a couple of days."

"Incidentally, take some cash. I'll give you a hint. It's parked in short-term parking. You've run up a pretty good parking fee by now. Bye, you little shit!"

The crazy, sex-crazed bitch had somehow stolen my spare key and later, my truck. It could have been worse. She could have left it in Mexico with the keys in it. In that case, I would never would have seen it again.

Otis couldn't get off from work to take me to the airport to search for my car. I took the city bus. I went from bus to bus asking questions and trying to figure out the routes. By the time I got to the airport, the temperature was over !00 degrees and it was past noon.

I couldn't wait for Otis' day off because without my truck, my lawn business was shut down. I had to find that truck today.

It was almost sundown when I found the truck. The ticket was over the visor and I owed 168 dollars to get it out of the airport. That left me with 18 dollars cash to my name.

Where had she gone? It was empty of gas, too. I've learned one thing about crazy women. They all want to get the last word, the last parting shot. I rue the day I got involved with any of them. I put the entire balance of my remaining cash in gas and drove back to my apartment.

Home was a welcome site. Hopefully, with the feeling that she got the last laugh on me, Deena would leave me alone. Peanut butter, crackers, and Ramen noodles would be my fare for the next few days, until I could take in some collections.

My next meeting with Hugh was a humble one. It did me good to laugh at my experience and made him laugh also. Luckily, he paid for our snacks and drinks. He had become my best friend, and I always looked forward to our brief meetings.

"The worst experiences make the best and funniest stories later," he said. "And it's not as much fun if you can't share with someone. I am just now able to talk about a crazy experience down in New Orleans. I ended up in jail with a D.U.I. I never thought I would get past that one."

"It's been a long while since I've had a D.U.I.," I said. What happened?"

"I was at a bar, working on a local chick, in a ritzy part of New Orleans near the Tulane campus. She was a beauty and was drinking me under the table. We were both snockered."

"We finally left to go to my hotel at about two o'clock in the morning. We were in her Jaguar convertible and I was driving. She was totally out of it. Then, not two blocks from the hotel, the ominous blue flashing lights came out of nowhere.

"I didn't know it at the time, but we were being filmed by the police cam. I put on my sober act and was telling the policeman that I had not been drinking and was in fact, the designated driver.

"Look officer, we're less than 2 blocks from the hotel. If you let us go, we'll go to our room and nobody will be the worse for it. See, here is my hotel key."

I tried to sound convincing, but it didn't help my cause that my new friend had taken her blouse off and it was on wrong side out when she was trying to tell the officer that I had not been drinking and that she had drunk only one beverage.

"Okay," he said, "get out and we'll do a test."

"I thought I had pulled it off, standing on one leg and walking the line."

"Mr. Farnsworth," he said, "you just take this breathalyzer test and with any luck, you can go back to the hotel."

I had always heard never to blow into the breathalyzer, if there is any chance that you think that you won't pass. I had lost count of the many drinks I had imbibed that night."

"Thanks officer, but that's not necessary. I've passed all your tests and I really need to be getting back. I have appointments early in the morning. Thanks for your time and have a good night."

"Mr. Hugh, you have a choice. You can take the test and if you pass it, you are free to go. If you don't take the test, or take it and fail, I'll be taking you both downtown. You'll have to reschedule your appointments. What will it be?"

"Will, I knew that my alcohol level was extremely high. If I blew into the device, that fact would be confirmed and there would never be a way to fight the D.U.I. ticket at a later date. Either way, I was going straight to jail."

"Officer, I don't believe in the integrity of those devices. If you don't let me go now, I'll have to ride downtown with you. I'm a man of my principles."

"Yes, Mr. Farnsworth, I can see that. Both of you come with me."

"With that, he handcuffed us both and we rode in the back of his car downtown and were booked, she with public drunkenness and lewdity, and me with driving while intoxicated."

"Wow, Hugh, I was going to say that was a close one and ask you how you got out of it. But I can see that you got busted. I once spent two weeks in the slammer one time for spanking my wife. It was no fun. So, what happened next?"

"It was horrible. I was booked and thrown in a large cell with local drunks and criminals. There was only one other person in jail with a suit and tie. He was a lawyer from Atlanta. His situation was similar to mine. He told me that it would be near impossible to get the ticket off of my record.

"I didn't blow into the breathalyzer." I said. "There is no hard evidence that my alcohol was illegally over the limit."

"You might try fighting it. I've seen it done with little success. It is expensive and the odds are not in your favor, especially if the officer had his car camera on. The video will be shown to a judge and jury."

I called my wife.

"Honey, I've gotten into a situation. I was at a bar after dinner with clients and had two drinks. An overzealous policeman stopped me and took me to jail. He didn't even give me a chance to take the breathalyzer."

"I'll be home Monday morning. I just wanted to keep you informed. I don't think anything will come of it.

"I stayed in jail until Monday morning. I cancelled all my appointments for the week and went home, trying out story after story to convince my wife and kids that I was totally innocent.

"I don't know what happened to my little friend. They impounded her car. She was in a heap of trouble, also. Did I mention that she was married?

"I spent the rest of the week lining up my lawyer and cashing in my savings for his retainer. He said we would fight it in court and hope for the best results."

"So, was your lawyer able to get you off?"

"No, Will, another factor entered into the equation and I opted for paying the ticket and letting it stay on my record. My lawyer subpoenaed the video and invited me to his office to view it."

What my attorney told me left me in a dilemma. "Hugh," he said, "the video is damning. You were slurring your words, stumbling around, and your topless girlfriend wasn't helping your cause. If you believe in miracles, I'll take your money and go forward with this. Your chances would be just about as good as you winning the lottery.

"Winning the case, which I probably wouldn't, wasn't as important as having my wife and daughter and her family seeing the video. I couldn't let them see it. It would have ended in a divorce, which I determined quickly would be costlier than the D.U.I. on my record. I had to pay the fines and take a different route.

"I had a new plan: I was to find Jesus.

"I became remorseful and repentant, 'born again,' as they say. I was talking about Jesus and redemption and going to church with my entire family. They gathered around me for support and said they would support me in every way to get me through this troubled time. I could not let them ever see that video. It worked at the expense of having a D.U.I on my record.

"I've been going to church every Sunday ever since. My family still supports me, but now there is an underlying trust issue to contend with."

"But you're still going to the bars," I said.

"Yes, Will, that is what I do. This is my nature. There is a predator somewhere in my DNA. I'm a good husband and a good father. The thing is, I like to screw around. Some would not understand my plight.

"One thing I can tell you for sure. I don't drive when I drink. If I get another D.U.I., I would lose my cushy job. Staying home in Texas all the time would be a fate worse than death.

"If I can't find a willing woman in my hotel bar, then I give up and call it a night. So far, my new plan has been working."

"Hugh, in some crazy way, you're still my hero. You have had more girlfriends being married than any single man I have ever known. You live the life that most men dream about."

"Will, sometimes, I would like to forget all about the life I have now and move to Mexico. I have an old college buddy that gave up all life as he knew it and cashed out and moved to Mexico."

"People thought he was crazy at the time. He's been there over 10 years and loves it. He lives like a king in a mansion. He has maids, gardeners, and drivers. And best of all, women at his fingertips.

"It would be a last resort measure if it happened. If it ever happens, you can come join me. From what I understand, it's not a bad life. I may want a friend down there."

"Hugh, I'd like that, but that takes money and money is the one resource that I have always been short of. If I win the lottery, I'll come down with you."

I gave up on meeting women after my incident with the nympho from San Francisco and after hearing Hugh's sad story. I wasn't having as much fun as before, but I was making and saving money.

I enjoyed my visits with Hugh. He has more charm and charisma than anyone I have ever known. He has lived a life so very different from my own: a full life, a life of his own choosing. He has opened my eyes to a window of dreams, that I would never have dared to fathom without his influence.

*   *   *   *   *

Meanwhile, Manuel and Antonio were still with me. We had acquired so many yards now that we were having to turn down new business. Both men were sending money to their respective families back in Guatemala. Manuel was saving enough to someday open a convenience store in Antigua, Guatemala.

Antonio was sending money to his fiancé and mother of his daughter in the same city. Both had goals and were working hard to achieve them. I admired their tenacity and ability to save so much of their income.

Chapter 7
The Family Reunion

One day, Otis surprised me with some news.

"Well, brother, things have been going well for the two of us. I've decided to give you your freedom and move out. I think that by now, each of us could handle paying for our own apartments."

"Are you moving back to Texas?" I asked.

"Hell no, are you kidding? I'll never go back except to visit Mama every once in a while. I wish I could get her to move out here near us. Maybe she could stay with Aunt Jinks and help her out. Aunt Jinks is getting pretty feeble now."

"If Aunt Jinks didn't have the horse races to go to every week, I don't think she would have a purpose in life. She said the horse races and your weekly lunch with her is the only thing she has to live for. Maybe she and Mama could keep each other company."

"Anyway, I'm getting my own apartment near here. I've been thinking. Do you remember your promise to buy Mama the Toyota pickup truck?"

"Yes, don't remind me. Promises are easy to make, hard to keep. I have some savings now, but not nearly enough to buy a new Toyota pickup truck. Maybe someday. I think that Mama's happy now for just the fact that neither of us are sponging off of her anymore."

"She's pleased to know that we're both finally on our feet financially. Now there are only Gordon and Freddie to bleed her of her social security checks. It's good to know that they both finally have jobs. I've heard that Gordon's new wife has a cushy bank job."

"Will, have you ever thought that Gordon and Freddie are doing us a service? Mama is not getting any younger and they are there to look after her. By both brothers living in Podunk, it takes a burden off of us. Have you thought of that?"

"No, I haven't. I find it hard to see it that way."

"Will, I've been driving by that "Tote the Note" used car lot and saw a white Toyota Corolla. Yesterday I stopped and asked about it. It's low-milage and only 4 years old.

"What do you think of going in together and buying it for Mama. It's not a pickup truck, but it looks like a better car than she's ever driven."

"Otis, you surprise me sometimes. That is a great idea. How much are they asking? I would rather pay cash if we can, than to pay the high interest notes. I've heard that they sometimes sell the same car several times, from financing them, and then repossessing them over and over."

"I've got $2,000 that I could pay towards the car," Otis said. "If you can cough up $4,000, I think we could swing the deal. Mama would think that we've won the lottery or robbed a bank."

We drove to the lot. A 400 lb. man with dark sunglasses walked out on the hot car lot to greet us.

"Hi! My name is Tommy. What can I put you into today? You know, you are lucky, we've just reduced prices on our entire inventory."

"Tommy, we're interested in the white Toyota facing the street. How much are you asking for that beauty?" I asked.

"We're giving that beauty away for just $7,000.00, he said. It's just been repossessed. If we hadn't collected so much from the last buyer, we would have to ask more for it.

"I haven't seen a deal like that in years. Come on in. No credit history is too bad for us to sell you that beauty."

"It's for our mom back in Texas. We didn't want to buy it on credit. We've got cash, but not enough to buy it."

"How much cash do you have?" Tommy asked, getting right to the point.

"We've got $6,000.00 cash between us," Otis said. "Maybe we can save up another thousand and come back. Hopefully, it won't be gone."

"Now Little Man, just hold your taters. My boss is in a rare, generous mood today. You should have seen the deal earlier today that he accepted for cash. I think that his wife has gone on a shopping spree and got him in Dutch. Let me go ask him how close he can get to your offer."

Tommy lumbered back to the tiny, air-conditioned hut in the middle of the car lot. In less than a minute, he returned.

"Well, boys, I've never seen my boss do anything like this before, but he is going to take your offer of $6,000.00 on this white beauty. You just have to pay for tax and tags."

"Tommy, when we say we have just $6,000 to spend on a car, that is our grand total. We'll just have to come back another day, or shop for an older car somewhere else."

"Look, you little cowboys," Tommy said. "Let Tommy go to bat for you. I'm going to do my level best to get that car for you for your $6,000 cash."

Tommy walked back into the hut, and hardly had time to explain our predicament when he came right back out with the keys to the car.

"Boys, Ol' Tommy never lets a good deal die. I've talked the boss into selling that Toyota for $6,000 drive-out. I'm going to throw in a $20 dollar bill just so you can take your mom out to lunch when you give her the car. I guarantee you she'll be one happy woman, and proud to have such handsome, generous sons."

Tommy started laughing so hard that we couldn't figure out what he said that seemed so funny to him.

We drove our Corolla to the apartment and shined the car up like a new dime. It was time to take a week's vacation and deliver Mama's gift of a lifetime to her in person. I hadn't been back to Texas in years and looked forward to seeing my old reprobate friends.

It was in the autumn of the year when Otis and I set out for Texas. Otis drove the Toyota and I drove my pickup truck. Mama knew we were coming but didn't know about her special gift. We were to leave the car with Mama and drive back together in my pickup truck.

For our little family reunion, Mama threw out all the stops. "My prodigal sons have returned," she said when she greeted us. "When did you get this new little fancy car?" she asked.

"It is a gift for you from the two of us." said Otis. Mama was stunned speechless as were Gordon and Freddie. Gordon suddenly became angry. "Why weren't Freddie and I told about the gift? We would have wanted to contribute too."

Otis replied, "Gordon, you've never had a penny to your name that Mama didn't give you in the first place. We didn't want this gift to be something that she had to pay any part of herself."

"Why you skinny little bastard!"

The fight was on. Gordon lunged at Otis with a body slam that put a hole in the sheetrock of Mama's living room. I got up and held Gordon back as Otis recovered. Gordon was filled with rage and uncontrollable.

Gordon slung me away like a rag doll and swung wildly at Otis. Otis ducked, then delivered a punch that whacked Gordon so hard in the jaw that he went out like a light and collapsed on the floor. Mama was screaming!

Freddie wasn't sure whose side to take so he watched the whole show without getting up from his seat.

Otis and I dragged Gordon outside and set him up on Mama's old La-Z-Boy on her front porch that Uncle Charlie had given her years ago.

"I can't believe you boys. You've ruined our precious family reunion. A mother should never have to watch her grown boys fist fight."

"Don't cry, Mama. Gordon has always been a hothead and a mooch. His time was due. He'll be all right."

Gordon's wife, Bunny Jo, had just arrived with dessert. When she saw Gordon knocked out on the La-Z-Boy, she dropped her pecan pie in the dirt.

"I demand to know what you've done to my husband," she screamed. Mayhem began again, just as we had gotten Mama calmed down. I walked her outside and explained.

"Bunny Jo, I know that you will find this hard to believe, but Gordon started a fight with Otis over the car we're giving to Mama. Things got out of hand and Gordon was knocked unconscious during the melee. He will be all right when he comes to. I've seen it before. I can help you get him home now if you want."

"Will, Gordon has always been a hothead. Sometimes he has been hard to live with. Yes, if you can help me get him back home, I'll take care of him."

It took all of us to drag Gordon back to Bunny Jo's car and put him in. We then had to follow Bunny Jo home so that we could unload Gordon and put him back in his own recliner, outside on the front porch. I could see that Otis could really pack a punch.

We returned to Mama's house, all but Bunny Jo and Gordon. Otis was nursing what seemed to be a bruised rib and black eye, but other than that, and some upcoming repairs to the house, things were back to normal.

"Mama, you have to laugh about it. What's a Perch family reunion without a fist fight or two?" I said.

Mama managed a little laugh through her tears. "Yes, I guess you're right. How did you ever save enough money to buy me such a nice gift? You boys are really thriving out west," she said.

"Are there any payments I will need to be making on the car?"

"No, Mama, the car is paid for, free and clear. You'll only need to change the oil once a year," Otis said. It should last you at least 10 years."

It was heart-rending to see Mama cry. "I love you boys. Now let's celebrate and go out for dessert. Maybe Gordon will have cooled off and, hopefully, will join us. His short temper tantrums usually don't last long. He explodes, then is over it."

We drove to the Dairy Queen, and all had ice cream, while the pecan pie, which I really preferred, was left in Mama's front yard in the dirt.

"Mama, I think we'll be going back to Arizona in the morning. We don't want to wear out our welcome, and we don't know what mood Gordon and Bunny Jo will be in when he wakes up. I have a feeling he won't be any too happy and it might be better for everyone if we're not around."

"I understand," Mama said. "Thank you, thank you, thank you so much for the precious gift. You boys are the best."

"Well, don't tell that to Gordon, it might cause another fistfight," quipped Otis, forcing a laugh, but not getting one from Mama.

We drove by Merci's early the following morning to say hello and eat a final taco breakfast before we left for our return trip to Phoenix.

"Buenos dias, Mijo, where have you been all this time? I've missed my favorite little vaquero."

"Merci, Otis and I are living in Arizona now. We're both working and life is good to us now."

"Otis doesn't look like life has been good to him with the black eye," she joked. "The tacos are on the house for you two."

"Merci, thank you, that is nice, but we have money now. You'll never have to sell us tacos on credit, ever again."

"You haven't forgotten about my little niece in Mexico have you? She is still available. Are you ready for me to make an introduction?"

"No, Merci, I am still not ready. I will surprise you someday and ask for her address and go down to see her, but only when I am ready."

"Adios, mijos, vaya con Dios! And don't forget about your friend, Merci."

"I'll never forget you. Bye, Merci."

With that, we drove west together in my pickup truck. "You can never go home again said some famous writer. He was right. At least, not without getting into a fist fight, right Otis?"

"You right, you right about that, Brother."

We arrived in Phoenix, deadheading the 750-mile drive in one long day. We took turns driving and counting the rest breaks and lunch and dinner, it took us 13 hours.

We were beat when we arrived. I drank a beer and took an Advil. Otis smoked a joint, and we went straight to bed, out like a light.

The next day, I met up with Manuel and Antonio. They were caught up with the yards and eager to get paid. It was time to seed winter rye in the lawns. The winter rye kept the yards green in the winter and also kept us in work mowing during the slower months.

It was nice to get back to normal life, such as it was. Otis had been given several raises in the super store cutting meat and was an assistant manager of the department. He was raking in the dough.

My yard business was thriving. After a few months of work, I had already saved what I had spent on Mama's car. My little life was going well. I had not seen nor heard from my friend Hugh Farnsworth in a long time.

After a few months, I couldn't stand it any longer, so I called Hugh.

"Hey, Hugh! Where have you been all this time? I hope you're not shacked up with some floozie who has stolen your money," I joked.

"Will, Old Hugh has come into hard times. I've had hell to pay lately. My world has turned upside down."

"What happened?" I asked.

"My wife became suspicious after the incident with the D.U.I. She hired a private detective to follow me. It didn't take him long to bust me. He has pictures of me that I have no idea how he could have gotten. His pictures are more incriminating than the D.U.I. video ever was. Now, she's filing for divorce and my daughter won't talk to me."

"Damn, that's terrible," I said. "Did you move out?"

"I had to," Hugh replied. "She had the locks changed on our home and won't let me back in."

"Déjà vu," I said.

"Where are you living?" I asked.

"I'm living in the hotels. I extended my accounts so that my company can pay for my time in hotels during the 4 weekdays. I have to pay for the weekends in hotels with my own personal credit card. She has frozen my bank accounts, and I can't get to my own money. I know this won't end well."

"I know the feeling and suffer your pain more than anyone else, as it all has happened to me first-hand. How do you see this playing out?"

"That's not the worst of it. I went to my doctor and have been diagnosed with colon cancer. It seems that the Lord has punished me twofold for my wayward discretions."

"You put that thought out of your mind. You'll get through this. At least you have your job. That's the most important thing."

"Thanks, Will, but even my job now is in jeopardy. They found out about my D.U.I. and have kept me out of the loop about aspects of the business that they always used to keep me abreast on. No Will, things are not good now."

"I feel your pain, but I know you'll get past all this. Try to stay positive."

"Here's something else. I called my job headhunter, just in case I were to get fired, and told him to be on the lookout for a job opening similar to this one. I've found that it's easier to find a job if you already have a job. Employers are suspicious of unemployed sales executives."

"Now that's a proactive move. You might just get a better job than you have right now," I tried to sound as comforting as I could.

"Well, here's what he found. He said that he has notice of a new job opening that would fit me perfectly. It's exactly like the job that I have now.

"I think it is the job I have now. He didn't name the company, but I think it's my own company trying to find a salesman to hire to replace me."

"Hugh, I doubt that. You've made a lot of sales for that company. A good salesman that produces can get away with almost anything. I doubt they would fire you.

"Tell me about your cancer. It's a cold-hearted woman who would kick a man out just as he is diagnosed with cancer."

"It can happen and has happened. My company's health insurance is paying for my cancer treatments. I think that the only reason they haven't fired me already, is because I have cancer and they're afraid that I'll sue them if I can link my cancer to being fired."

"Damn, that's tough. How far advanced is your cancer?"

"They caught it early and said that the odds are in my favor. I have been responding well to treatments, they say. I have to take both radiation and chemotherapy."

"I'm so sorry to hear this. It goes to show that a man can be on top of the world one month, and in the shithouse the next one. Can you get together for a drink?" I asked.

"Yes, I'd like that, except now, I can't drink," he replied.

"Okay, let's meet for dinner. You're still paying, I hope. They haven't taken that expense account away have they?"

"No, I still have it to entertain clients, but we had probably better plan it sooner than later. I'll see you next Friday night at Santangelos."

"You're on," I said. "See you there at 7:00 p.m. on Friday."

I hardly recognized Hugh when he came through the door. His once muscular body had been decimated by his cancer treatments. There was something different about his hair, too. He was wearing a toupee, similar to the one I took off of Mr. Burns, and he had shaved his once-thick mustache.

"You look great," I said as he approached the table.

"You are not a good liar," he said. "I know I look like shit."

He did look like shit, but I wasn't going to tell him that.

"Hugh, you are the experienced one here, but I have some advice for you. It's from knowledge from doing things the wrong way. You need to be as strong and resolute as you can be now."

"What do you mean?"

"Fight your wife for half of everything you have, including cars and furniture. I was given counsel, by my Uncle Charlie, to give in on everything on my divorce, and my wife would be generous.

"Hugh, it was the worst mistake ever. She took every penny from me and was no happier than if I had stood firm for my half. After all these years, she would still kill me if she could get away with it.

"Stand firm for what is yours!"

"I'll remember that," Hugh said as he walked away. I noticed that he lumbered like an old man. Last year, he was strutting like a rooster. His clothes now hung loose on him like a homeless person.

That was the same week that I got news about Uncle Charlie. The news came to me on my weekly call from Mama.

"Will, I have some sad news. Your Uncle Charlie has cancer. I didn't know it but he's had it for a while. I don't remember what kind it is, but it is one of the bad ones."

"Mama, none of them are good. It couldn't happen to a nicer guy."

"Now Will, you shouldn't wish cancer on anyone."

"Oh, I can think of several people whom I would wish it on. I hope he can get cured. Sometimes it happens. It just so happens that I just found out that my best friend here in Phoenix has cancer."

"I didn't know this either, but his Charmy has left him. His daughter won't have anything to do with him either."

"Where have I heard this before? What happened?"

"It seems that he was carrying on with a woman or two in the furniture stores when he was traveling. I can't believe his wife would leave him after all those years, after all he has given to her and his daughter."

"Hmm....I could give him some advice. Give up everything you have to your ex-wife and see if she will be generous. Then he will have cancer and be penniless. Ol' Uncle Charlie didn't practice what he preached."

"Will, Uncle Charlie has been very good to us. Don't talk like that."

"Yes, while he was on top of the world, he left us some bread crumbs to do his cleaning and watching over one of his places. I can't get past his leaving me in jail to rot, and then firing me while I was still locked up."

"Will, if he had bailed you out, you wouldn't be where you are now. You seem happier than you've ever been. Sometimes the Lord works in mysterious ways. By the way, my car runs perfectly. All my neighbors are impressed that you two boys gave it to me free and clear. Thanks again.

"You should call your Uncle Charlie. I'm sure he would like to hear from you. It would cheer him up."

"I'll think about it." I said. "By the way, who was he cavorting with when he got caught?"

"I'm not sure, I think it was someone in one of the stores that you had worked in."

"Interesting," I said. "I would sure like to check out his neck ties."

"What are you talking about?" she asked.

"Oh nothing, I've got to go now. Bye, Mama."

"Will, call him. Bye."

A few days later, my guilty conscious got the better of me. It wouldn't have happened, except for the fact that my new best friend is suffering from cancer. I had to look up Uncle Charlie's phone number as I had forgotten it with the many years.

"Hello, Uncle Charlie. This is Will Perch. Do you have a few minutes?"

"Why, hello Will. You don't know how great it is to hear from you. I was afraid that you might have carried a grudge."

"Why would you say that?" I asked. "You mean for letting me rot in jail and then firing me, and afterwards for the terrible advice you told me to take during my divorce? No, Uncle Charlie, I never think about it."

"Will, I look back and regret some of the things I've done. I realize that I did the same things that I fired you for. For that, I'm sincerely sorry."

"Uncle Charlie, do you need any advice regarding your divorce settlement?"

"No, Will, I'm sorry for that, also. I was hoping we might be friends. My kids won't talk to me now."

"I know the feeling. Okay, Uncle, we are friends."

"Thanks, Will, you don't know how much that cheers me."

"Bye, Uncle Charlie. Come see me in my little apartment when you recover. I'll pay for dinner."

Sometimes there is justice in the world, even if it is poetic justice. It's rare, but sweet when it occurs.

I continued with my yard business. Manuel and Antonio had another friend that I hired. My business was spanning northern Phoenix. I rented space in an industrial park and staged my equipment and repair work there.

It was easy to get enough business to warrant the third person. More money was coming in. There was more to look after which kept me busy.

It was only a few months later that out of the blue, I heard a rap on the door. Chills ran down my back as I thought back to Deena. I was hesitant to open the door.

There was old Uncle Charlie. Old is the operative word here. He had his carry-on luggage with him. He was a skeleton of the man I used to know.

"Uncle Charlie, is that you? I hardly recognized you. You're a sore sight for eyes."

"Yes, I was wondering if I could stay for a while. I have some golfing buddies in Scottsdale I've known for a long time back. I can't play golf anymore but they invited me out to go play with them. I can still drive a cart."

"Sure, Uncle Charlie. Otis has his own place. I'll invite him over and we'll go out to dinner together. Stay as long as you want."

I made the invitation without believing he would take me so literally on it. Uncle Charlie stayed for six weeks. I gave him a key and went about my daily business. He had arranged to have his medical treatments in a Phoenix hospital.

He was a good house guest. He stayed in his room and read. He went out with his golf buddies occasionally, but the outings wore him out.

"I'm going to beat this cancer," he said. "I've always achieved what I set out to do if I was determined to do so."

"Uncle Charlie. You're not my boss any longer and you're staying in my home, humble though it is, for free. I feel that I can be candid.

"You will not beat this cancer. Better men than you have not beaten it. You will probably find the concept of death a relief before your bout is over. You need to consider a plan of action from that angle. It would be wise for you to get your affairs in order.

"It's none of my business, but you have to put on your practical hat, and go on with the rest of your life accordingly. Once you have your exit plan, you can relax and live your last days in peace."

"You are a negative little shit," Uncle Charlie replied. "I ought to leave right now."

"Don't let the door hit you on the ass on the way out," I said. "You can stay as long as you want, and you can leave whenever you like."

"You are right," he said. "I have been living a life of delusion since my recent bout of bad luck. Go get me a cold beer, and open one for yourself."

I brought the icy cold beer to Charlie. "Before I give this to you, are you sure you want to drink it given your condition?"

"Hell yes, and while you're at it, roll me a joint. I want to enjoy myself tonight."

"Wow! Uncle Charlie, I've never seen this side of you. I'll call Otis to bring over some 'primo'."

"What's that?" he asked.

"You'll see."

Otis's little eyes opened as wide as saucers when he saw Uncle Charlie on my easy chair drinking a beer.

"Brother, roll 3 j's, one for each of us. We're having a family party."

We talked into the night, each telling funny stories of our past. It was past midnight when we all hit the sack.

I left early to meet my workers and line up the work for the week. When I returned at the end of the day, Uncle Charlie was gone. On his bed was a note and a hundred-dollar bill.

> Good-bye my little friend. I want you to know that I have enjoyed my stay immensely. You've helped me to see myself as I have never been able, in the past.
>
> Good luck to you and Otis. I am proud of you and the lives that the two of you have made for yourselves.
>
> Bye,
> Uncle Charlie

My hate for Uncle Charlie was gone. I didn't think him a good person any more than before. His recent visit with me didn't change the fact that he had been a greedy bastard most of his life. But my hate for him was gone.

It is strange but my soul felt liberated. I now wish I had forgiven him years ago, not because he deserved it, but because of what it would do for me.

In my next meeting to see Hugh, I told him about my houseguest.

"Damn, Will, you're a better man than I am for being nice to the old coot. I would have politely declined and kicked him in the ass."

I didn't tell Hugh that I couldn't do that because they both looked so old and weak from the ravages of their respective diseases.

"I did it for Mama, not Uncle Charlie," I said. "Mama thinks that he has been good to her through the years, throwing her a few crumbs every now and then. I let him stay with me as a favor to her."

"No, I have not forgotten how he treated me in my younger days, when I was down and out in Texas and Kansas. Personally, Hugh, the whole scenario just seems like a bad dream that I'll probably someday forget."

"Down and out in Podunk, Texas. That would be a good name for a book." Hugh laughed. "I may have some good news. The doctors say that I may not have to go in for additional treatments. There's a chance that the radiation and chemotherapy has done its work. Only time will tell."

"That's great. We have to celebrate our small victories when we get them. You may not want to tell me, but how is your divorce proceeding coming along, and your work situation."

"The divorce is a mess. Luckily, Texas is a no-fault divorce state, and our assets are to be split half and half. She thinks that the law should read otherwise and is spending money on attorneys to tell her what she wants to hear. I will be happy with my half. I need not be in a hurry, but when the dust settles, I'll have my half, or close to it, and go on my merry way."

"As far as work, things are not good there either. I have another lawyer sending letters to see that I do not get fired until I have my cancer completely treated. After that, I would wager that I will become unemployed. Do you have any openings in your grass cutting business?"

"I do, but even if you were healthy, you wouldn't last a week, working with the Guatemalans. You would do best to get a good settlement from your divorce."

"By the way, how much do you figure that it'll take to live in Mexico?" I asked. "You never know when a bump in the road might lead you to a happier life. It could be now is the time for you to move."

"I don't know." Hugh replied. "One needs enough, but what is enough? That is the question that no one has an answer to. I don't want to go down there and outlive my money."

"Maybe enough is whatever you have. Don't you think you can adjust your lifestyle to whatever money you have coming in? Your 'enough' would be much more than my enough."

"Stop with this philosophical crap. Let me ask you the most important question. Have you gotten any strange nookie lately?"

"Hugh, If I got any at all, it would be strange. No, since the episode of Deena and the stolen truck, I have kept my body parts inside my pants. I miss it sometimes, but my forays into sexual delight always have ended in misery.

"Maybe someday when I think I can afford a setback, I'll try again, but not now. The balance of making a living is too delicate. I can't afford for anything to go wrong now."

"I may have to give it up also, I don't know if the body parts will work after all that I will have gone through with my treatments."

"There is much more to life than strange nookie."

"There is?" Hugh looked incredulously at me. "I have to leave on that one. See you next month."

"Is this what the beginning of old age is, watching your friends and family become sick and frail?" I began to realize that my life was more than half over, and that was supposedly the best half.

I hadn't done much for fun during the first half, and the second half didn't seem to be faring any better, except that I was more comfortable financially.

Maybe it was because I was lonely, maybe it was because the fact that people I've known well were being stricken with health problems, and maybe it was just because I wanted to have a good story to entertain Hugh at our next meeting that I decided to explore the dating sites on the world wide web once again.

By the end of the day, I found a dating site called 'findyourlatinlove.com." I had nothing to lose by joining so I posted a picture and wrote a bio.

I didn't lie about my age or height. Women always eventually find out and better if they think you didn't lie in the first place.

About two weeks into my search, I met Marcela from San Carlos.

Chapter 8
Marcela

My yard work kept me too busy to spend much time trying to find companionship. I was limited to about an hour at night before I was down and out from a hard day's work.

"Why don't you meet women the old-fashioned way, like everybody else?" Otis asked one evening while he was visiting after his work. "Go to a bar. It is quicker and you see the other person in person."

"Unlike my friend Hugh, I don't have free resources for drinks, which is always expected. I don't have the time when I get home from work. After I shower in the evening, I'm only good for an hour or two before I'm dead asleep.

"'Slow' works for me if I can find the right person," I answered.

I had picked up some Spanish from my co-workers. Within a week, I received a message from Marcela in San Carlos, Mexico.

Marcela knew a little more English than I knew Spanish. We exchanged information and with time got to know each other. Finally, it was time for us to meet in person.

During this time that I was communicating with Marcela, on Hugh's advice, I got a passport. I was to learn that the passport was my ticket, not only into Mexico, but to countries all over the world.

The day came when I bought two road maps and headed down south. The drive to San Carlos was over 8 hours. I stretched it to 10 hours, getting lost a few times, and finding my way back on the route.

On my long drive down, I asked myself, "Am I crazy for going to Mexico to find a girlfriend, when there are over 150 million women in the USA?" It sounded foolish, even to me, but the plan was in motion and I was on my way. I wanted to see how it would play out.

We met in a restaurant called La Palapa on the Sea of Cortez. I had not fathomed how beautiful that a beach and sea scene could be. I realized that my little life had limited me from the nicer things and places in the world.

Marcela was waiting for me at a table at the restaurant when I arrived. She was, or at least seemed to me, to be the most beautiful woman I had ever known. She had a young voice and a sweet smile.

"You are more short than I thought you would be."

"I didn't lie about my height. Look it up. If you are not interested, you can leave now. I'll just stay and play on the beach for a while."

"Oh no, mi chico rubio, you look nice, being short is no problem for me. I like the short men."

"Okay, thanks for that." I answered.

We had lunch and a drink. The setting was perfect. I could see why Hugh's friend loved living in Mexico. Maybe Hugh could move down here and invite me over some time to visit. The lifestyle is way too tempting to stay very long. It was too easy to forget about life in the real world back home.

Conversation flowed smoothly. The next day, Marcela and I frolicked on the beach, taking time to grab a margarita and lie together in the hammock. I couldn't remember having such a fun time.

I could see why Hugh's friend loved living in Mexico. The life south of the border is way too expensive for my paltry savings to afford. Still, it was a nice, new subject for a daydream. Marcela guided me around the city while I drove. It seemed to me a paradise.

Maybe Otis was right. A man doesn't have to settle with the likes who have been my wives. I was excited about a relationship for the first time in years. Before it was time for me to return to Phoenix, we were already discussing the possibility of her coming to Phoenix and staying with me.

"Adios y que te vaya bien," she said as I drove away. I was determined to learn more Spanish at that time.

Meanwhile, back in Phoenix, I was needed to conduct my work. The boys did all right for a week or so if I were gone, but beyond that, problems occurred that had sometimes caused me to lose some of my regular accounts.

I had mowers to repair and some patching up to do with some of the clients. It was hard to balance keeping a relationship with staying ahead at work. I don't see how Hugh did it for so many years.

While I was up to my elbows in grease, I got a call from Otis.

"Hey, Will, you better come quick. Aunt Jinks just died. She was at the racetrack and just collapsed."

I was dumbstruck and grief-stricken. I got in my truck and rushed over. I began crying for the first time in years. As I wiped my tears with my greasy hands, my face took on the countenance of a raccoon by the time I arrived.

Cousins whom I had never met were gathered at Aunt Jink's home. As I tried to make friendly, the soap I used to clean the grease from my face changed my countenance from the raccoon to the zombie. Aunt Jinks would have thought it funny. None of her relatives did, however.

Aunt Jinks had won her last bet. It was a two-dollar win ticket bet that paid $81.00. The exhilaration of winning was evidently too much for her weak heart and she never collected her winnings. She died with the winning ticket in her hand. We felt it was the way she wanted to go out.

I had always admired her because she lived her life on her own terms. She refused to listen to the naysayers who would hold her back. She left Texas for the unknown, a chance for a better life, and never looked back. Because of her, I had done the same thing.

I owed so much to Aunt Jinks. Thanks to her, my little life had turned around years ago. It was sad to lose such a good friend. Rest in Peace, Aunt Jinks. Happy trails.

It was good for Otis and me to stay busy during that time following her services. It took our minds off of Aunt Jinks. I went back to repairing equipment and lining up work. I had just invested in a zero-turn mower and we were covering lawns at a record pace.

Business was good. In my spare time I connected with Marcela. We chatted online at least once a week. She wanted to move to Phoenix to be with me.

"Will, you're a smart man, but something happens to your reasoning around women. You need to start thinking with your head," Otis said to me one day.

"What do you mean?" I asked.

"Can't you see? Marcela is just after you to get her green card. Once she becomes legal in the U.S., you will never see nor hear from her again. And that is if you are lucky."

"A friend of mine at work did the same thing you're doing. His Latina honey took him for everything he had before she flew the coop."

"I'm sure she is sincere. She really cares for me."

"Yes, you and how many others?" Otis replied. "You should check with your friend Hugh, who is an expert on women, if you don't believe me. See what he has to say about it."

Sometimes in life, you meet the self-proclaimed experts who have a lot of advice but no experience in matters in which they advise you. Otis, who himself had never been in a long-term relationship with a woman, had been right in the past when advising me. I couldn't ignore his advice. It was time to meet up with Hugh and get his opinion.

"Hugh, you're looking better and this time, I'm not lying," I said as he entered the outdoor restaurant.

"I am doing better, physically," he said.

"The doctors said that there was no trace of the cancer now, and we would halt treatments until something shows up. He said to be cautiously optimistic."

"That's good news. My Uncle Charlie has a different cancer and may not be much longer in this world. You're lucky in this respect if you can call having cancer being lucky. What is happening on the divorce issue?"

"Well, we will be officially divorced early this coming summer. My settlement didn't go as well as I had hoped, but I'm glad I followed your advice. My crazy wife wanted everything. I had to fight and scratch for what I could get."

"It's what they do, when they find out what we do," I said.

"Men and women are just wired differently. Our DNA's cause us to do different things. When we mate for life, we're going against our natural instincts. In our society, we always pay the cost. It seems sometimes that women have made all the rules."

"You right, You right! Now order us a beer."

The beer was cold and tasty on our hot afternoon in the shade of the giant umbrella, outside on a hot, hot day. We sat for hours, eating chips and salsa, and drinking beer.

"How is work?" I asked. "Did things settle down? You really didn't need all these bad things happening to you at the same time."

"It hasn't gotten much better. The only good news is that I'm still there. I seem to be black-balled and my headhunter can't find anything else for me. I'll hang in as long as I can.

"I've already received notice that I will be terminated in June. I've been given the option to make it look like I resigned in order to find my next job more easily. My lawyer negotiated a one-year severance package for me. That should buy me the time I need to get my life on track again.

"If there is anything good about the whole predicament I'm in, it's that I will have all divorce proceedings to end and my part of my settlement. We didn't go after each other's pensions, so I'll have a little booster to get me through the golden years, if I live that long. I really don't know what I'll be doing if I can't get the next job."

"Hugh, I don't care what others may say, but I think that you're a smart man and I know you'll land on your feet. You've got a whole year to find something else. Don't give up on that Mexico dream.

"Speaking of Mexico, I have a question for you. I've gotten back on-line and met a little senorita from Mexico. She lives in San Carlos near the beach. I've already been down to see her."

"This is interesting. Tell me about her."

"We've met one time and have visited by phone and computer pretty regularly. Our visit went great. She is the prettiest woman I have ever known. Now she wants to come to the U.S.A. and move in with me."

"Wow, that sounds like things have moved quickly. I'd be careful if I were you. I've heard similar stories from people I've met in my travels. Sometimes it works, usually it doesn't. When it doesn't work, it never ends well."

"Funny, that's what Otis said. What's the worst that can happen?"

"There's a number of things that can occur that you've never thought about. Do you read?"

"What the hell are you talking about?"

"Do you read books for entertainment?"

"I've never read a book in my life since high school. Who has time to read?"

"I've just read *The Art of War*. It was written over a thousand years ago by a brilliant Chinese general. It was suggested by another drinking buddy who went through a divorce."

"The thing I got out of it was to know yourself, and to study and know your enemy, only then could you win. In your case, you don't know your enemy, and you can't trust yourself with the judgements you've made in the past. Without a little more knowledge, you're probably doomed."

"Will, Otis is right to be wary of women with evil intentions. But, on the other hand, if you don't go for it, you will grow old and regretful before your time. Just be careful."

"Hugh, that is not what I wanted to hear, but I'll keep that advice in mind and go forward in my relationship with my new senorita. I'm not getting any younger or better looking. This might be my last chance at romance."

"Good luck. Go home, and don't get caught by the police while driving. See you next time. Ciao."

"Ciao?"

"Adios!"

I walked into my apartment as my phone rang.

"Hola mi querido, when do you want me to visit you in your home? Do you miss your little novia?" she asked.

"Yes, I miss you, Marcela. What do you think of my coming to see you again in San Carlos? I think at this point, it might be easier," I replied.

"I want to see your home, how you live, meet your friends, and family," she said

"Marcela, I don't think that is a good idea. I work most of the time in the day. I am only home at night to eat dinner and clean up. My family is back in Texas, and I don't see them often. I don't have many friends. Our lives and culture are much different from in Mexico. I think you would get bored here pretty quickly."

"Maybe I can get a little job there too. Then I will not get bored. We can be together every night and have the weekends together."

"I can catch a bus to the border in Nogales. Meet me there and I'll ride with you to your home in your truck. How about this weekend?"

I wanted to see Marcela again. I enjoyed myself when I was with her. She was a lot of fun. On the other hand, the voices in my head told me to be careful. The voices sounded a lot like Otis and Hugh.

"Okay," I said to Marcela, "I'll come down and meet you at the border crossing in Nogales this Saturday. Can you meet me at 2:00 p.m.? We can be back by 6:00 p.m. in time to go to dinner. If you want, I can invite Otis."

"Si, si, I would like that. I will start packing. Will, I am so happy."

"I am also. Nos vemos on Saturday."

I worked during the week and spent the evenings cleaning my little apartment. I arranged for Otis to meet us at the apartment on Saturday at 6:00 p.m. My heart was racing, just thinking about our upcoming time together, and going into this relationship with eyes wide open.

"Do you have your condoms ready?" Otis asked. "Remember what I told you."

"Yeah, yeah, yeah," I said, "I'm covered."

"Famous last words were never spoken. You really need to get clipped."

"What do you mean?" I asked.

"If ever anybody needed a vasectomy, it is you," he answered. "Then you can play the rest of your life and not end up with yet a third child who will grow up to hate you like the other two."

"I'll think about it. It's too late now for this visit."

"I'll see what I can do," Otis said,

"What do you mean?" I asked.

"I'll tell you when I do it. It's a good thing that you got a rational friend in your corner, brother."

"Okay, thanks. I'll wait, but I don't like surprises."

"You will like this one."

The week passed quickly and it was time for us to meet. Marcela had a bag packed and was waiting for me at the border gate when I arrived. I picked her up and we ate bowls of Caldo de Res at Cocina La Ley. We visited the entire drive back to Phoenix, as the conversations flowed easily.

"Your apartment is smaller than I thought it would be," she said. "Don't you own your own business?"

"Mira, Marcela, In my little life, I mow lawns for a living. I have two workers. I don't know if that would be considered a business. This is where I live and I don't see moving anytime soon. If we are to have a future, you need to know my life."

"Oh, don't get me wrong," she said. "I like small apartments. They are easy to clean. I see you have a pool. We can go swimming every day."

"Yes, that sounds like fun—every day I'm not working, maybe. You can hang out at the pool while I'm at work."

Our visit was going well. Marcela made me breakfast and packed me a bean and potato burrito lunch every day. Manuel and Antonio were amused. I showed them a photo of us together.

"Does she want you for your looks or your money?" they asked, laughing hilariously. "Señor Jeffe, quedado, don't put her name on your bank account. Buenos suerte!"

Damned, even my Guatemalan workers were dubious of her. I watched her behavior closely.

Otis met us in our apartment for dinner. Marcella was a good cook. We had beans with fried plantain bananas, and beef carne de guisada. It was delicious.

"Put this in her coffee in the morning," Otis whispered to me. "It's a morning after pill and insures that Marcella won't get pregnant. I got them from my supplier."

"I don't think that's a good idea."

"Well, consider the ramifications if you don't." he said.

I considered my action devious, but with all my experience, caution seemed to win out. I did as Otis said.

Marcela didn't give me reason to rouse my suspicions. In three weeks, it was time to take her back to San Carlos.

We arrived in Mexico in time for a long weekend holiday. We frolicked on the beach and took naps on hammocks in the shade. I was in paradise. Life was more fun in Mexico than it was in the U.S.A. I didn't want it to end.

Still, I had to make a living. Living poor anywhere was no fun, and certainly not in Mexico. Extreme poverty was everywhere you looked. This fact kept me on a rigid course of keeping my business healthy.

Otis met me on my arrival back home.

"Will, you've had a surprise visitor. It's Deena from San Francisco."

A chill ran down my back and I was feeling faint.

"What did she say?" I asked.

"She was angry and disappointed that you weren't here to meet her. I took her to dinner and calmed her down. I hope you don't mind."

"She's gone now?" I asked.

"Yes, she's gone," Otis told me.

"Well, that's a relief. I don't need her in my life now while I'm trying to make things work with Marcela."

"Will, that's not all. She came with an ugly little boy in tow who looks a lot like you. She said the child is yours, and that you need to do the right thing."

My heart sank to my stomach. Where have I heard that before? I asked myself.

"I really don't want to have anything to do with her. When did she leave?"

"I have to be honest with you. She stayed in your apartment. I told her about your relationship with Marcela. She asked me to stay with her and the boy over the weekend."

It was hard to take everything in that I was hearing and feeling. Another child would not only doom my relationship with Marcela but wreck the rest of my life. I was not going to be forced to marry another woman that I didn't want to marry.

"What do you mean stay over?" I asked.

"I mean, it's just what you think it is. We spent the whole time together. She wants to see me again. What do you think? I won't do it if you don't want me to."

"Otis, she is crazy and devious. You don't know what you're getting yourself into. What do you think of her?"

"To be honest, I found her attractive and interesting. It's the first time in a very long time that I've gotten excited about someone."

"If you are attracted to her, it's fine with me. It seems like a pretty weird situation."

"So, with your blessings, I will consider seeing her again."

"Otis, you are my imperceptible savior. I don't know what I would do without you."

I was uneasy, as I prepared for my monthly meeting with Hugh.

"How are you and the little senorita getting along?" he asked. "Do you have a photo you could show me?"

I pulled out my wallet and displayed the picture I always carried.

"Hijole!" he said. "She is a beauty. Will we be hearing wedding bells ringing anytime soon?"

"That's what she wants. She's already pressuring me to sign documents that would allow her to stay past her tourist visa. I'm tempted to sign them."

"I don't blame you," he said. "You could certainly do worse than her in the looks department. Do you mind if I take a photo of your photo with my phone?"

"Go ahead."

Hugh still sported his oversized toupee but had gained some weight and was looking much better than before. It appeared that he was one of the few lucky ones to beat cancer.

"Besides your hair, do you have any effects of the chemo and radiation?" I asked.

"Will, I wouldn't tell everyone this, but I have neuropathy in my extremities. My fingers, my toes, and the other extremity. Do you know what I mean, Will?" he winked.

"It's ironic, that after all this time, and all the women I've known, in the Biblical sense, while I was married, now that I'm free and available, my equipment no longer operates."

"That's a shame. Will that come back?" I asked.

"Only time will tell." He said. "Karma has a cruel sense of humor. I know that the way I've lived my life has not been right. I deserve all that I get now."

"Don't talk like that." I answered. "You've been an inspiration to me. You'll bounce back. You've had a good run, and now experiencing a setback.

"I see a future for you living the dream in Mexico, near a beach somewhere, sipping Corona's all day, with your own Marcela. Everyone deserves a chance to be happy.

"I also have some other news," I said.

"You have a very interesting little life, he replied. What else is going on?"

"I've been reluctant to tell you but Deena came back to see me. She had a toddler with her that she claims is mine.

"Damn, Will, you are like a little sperm bank. Does this make 3 children that you have now?"

"It appears that way and get this. She came while I was in Mexico and called Otis. She and Otis seemed to hit it off, and they spent 3 days in my apartment, hardly coming up for air, I suppose."

"That is truly complicated," Hugh told me. "How do you feel about Otis and Deena being together."

"That's the strange part. They seem to be getting along really well. Otis wants to see her again. It's all fine with me. The thought of her has haunted my dreams ever since our last episode. With her finding a boyfriend, it takes the pressure off of me. On the other hand, I wouldn't want Otis to feel her wrath.

"In fact, if their relationship were to become harmonious, it could cause a big problem in my life to be solved, if they continue to get along well."

"That's just about the craziest story I've ever heard. If things work out for them, how would you feel about your brother raising your son?"

"I think it would be great. I would at least get to see him grow up, which I couldn't do with the other two wives."

"I'm truly amazed. Will wonders never cease?" Hugh replied. "Let me know how both scenarios develop, he said, and good luck with the senorita."

"Thanks, buddy, for the encouragement. I'll think about that. See you next time. Adios."

"Adios," Hugh responded.

"Ciao!" I said.

During my break from Marcela, I saw a Urologist and arranged to have the vasectomy, that both Hugh and Otis encouraged me to get.

As with many events in life that a person seriously dreads, I discovered that the procedure was easier and less painful than I had imagined it to be. I couldn't dance the boogaloo, or do much physical work, but I could get around just fine. In a week, I was almost healed. I wished that I had gotten it done years ago.

The courtship of Otis and Deena worked out better than anyone could have guessed. Otis was a natural with the boy, Henry, and Deena seemed to appreciate Otis more than she ever did me. Deena seemed to be in love with Otis. With her realization that her looks were fading, she latched onto Otis with a vengeance to make the union work.

I called Otis one morning during my morning break on a hot July day. It was out of the ordinary that I call him as I have never been one to call just to chat when work was at bay.

"Hey Otis! How are things going?"

"Will, good to hear from you. I'm glad you called. Things are great, man. I have some news. You won't believe this, but I'm going to quit my cushy job at the supermarket."

"What? Are you crazy?" I asked. "You've put in a long time at that store to work your way up to where you are now. You've gotten regular raises, have insurance, and some retirement built up. What is going on in that crazy, empty, red head of yours?"

"I'm moving to San Francisco. Deena, Henry, and I will be living in her cushy home on Knob Hill. Listen, it all makes sense. Between the two of us, she is by far the breadwinner. I could own the meat department at the store and not make what she is making at her Silicon Valley position.

"What I earn now, would not be much more than what she pays for childcare there. Besides, I'm ready for a little break. I've never been too industrious and this job sometimes gets me down. I've stayed with it for the same reason that every sad sack across the country stays with their job— to pay the bills.

"I think I'll enjoy the time off."

"What if it doesn't work out?" I asked.

"Will Perch, when you're near the bottom rung of the ladder, you don't have far to fall. If it doesn't work out, I'll walk away, and start all over. I feel, now, the same way that I felt when I left Texas. It feels right. I don't have much to lose by going, and I have a lot to gain.

I've already made my decision. Time for the next chapter, Bro!"

"Otis, I'll miss you and your worldly advice. Let's agree to stay in touch. The world is a smaller place than it used to be. With the new phones, we can email, text, and call without ever opening a computer.

"And for the record, and from now forever forward, the boy is yours and always has been. I'll only be as active in the boy's life as you want me to be."

"Will, it's a secret that the three of us will take to our graves. That's a deal.

"I'll contact you at least once a month. The same goes for you. Let me know how it goes with your little senorita from San Carlos."

Life is strange sometimes. When you're on top and get complacent, something will always come and knock your block off. And then, when you are in your darkest moment, for no reason, something will change and get your life back on track again.

Chapter 9
The Document

I was encouraged by the success of my younger brother's strange arrangement and was determined to make my relationship work with Marcela. I called her the very same evening.

"Hola! Marcela! Como te vas? I hope you've had a good day."

"O Si!" she replied. "I played on beach in the morning before it got too hot and bought some fish from the dock to bring home for dinner. I played on the computer in the afternoon. Si! Today was a good day.

"I saw my abogado yesterday. He gave me some papers for you to sign. I will bring them with me on my next visit. Will, it is very important that you sign them."

"Abogado? What is that?" I asked.

"He is my lawyer. The papers will make the path for us to get married, and for me to live in the U.S.A. We will be happy forever."

"Don't you want your novia to live with you?" she asked.

"Oh sure!" I tried to sound excited and convincing, while at the same time a chill of worry ran down my back."

"Can you come to the border this weekend?" she asked.

"Yes, I'll pick you at the regular place at the border gate."

Marcela had a gift for me, rather, for us, to celebrate our relationship. It was a bottle of Pueblo Viejo Tequila. We drank half of it on the way home. The other half was consumed while in the apartment complex's new hot tub. I can say this for Marcela. She can hold her liquor.

If only that hot tub could talk, what tales it could tell! Under the influence of a persuasive Latina and a horrendous hangover, I signed all the documents the next morning. I didn't read, nor could I, as it was written in Spanish.

The final page had to be executed in front of a notary. I figured I was safe as long as there was still her final signature to be both signed and witnessed.

"Señor Will, where can we find a notario in Phoenix? Do you know of one?"

"Marcela, I do not know of a lawyer. But if it is only a notary stamp you want on the signature, almost any bank can provide it. I'll check."

"Mi amor, it needs to be done today. Many things written in the contract must be done in a timely manner. Can you go to your bank today?"

"I guess so. I have to get work lined up and I will take you to the bank at noon."

"Are you Will Perch," asked the banker. "I will need to see some identification."

"I have a passport and a driver's license," I replied.

"Will, are you aware that this document is written in Spanish? Do you know what it says?"

"No, not really. I don't speak much Spanish. I'll sign it anyway."

"That's not very smart. I could probably find a translator within a week and get you a copy in English. You should really know what you're signing."

"No!" piped up Marcela. "Many parts of the contract depend on the signatures very soon! Will, tell her you will sign it because you trust your Marcela!"

I had a headache that wouldn't stop, like two hot iron rods going through my temples to the back of my cranium.

"Okay, I will sign now, and get the English copy later," I said. Tell me where to sign. I don't feel well and need to go home."

The execution of the documents was completed. Marcela deposited the originals into her leather valise.

"Now, we can live happy forever. I can get a job."

The coming days passed easily and happily. I worked just the same with the boys, but Marcela was waiting at the end of the day with a 'south of the border' dinner.

She wanted a computer of her own and I promised to buy her one when I had saved up the extra funds. Meanwhile she used my computer.

As time went on, I found her to be on my computer most of the day.

"Marcela, who are you writing to all of these hours?"

"I'm writing to my Mommi and Poppi back in San Carlos. Don't worry about my time on the computer. I clean your clothes and cook your meals every day. I am a good wife."

I didn't correct her, but I became more suspicious as time went on, as to what she did on the computer all day. Finally, over a week later, the bank lady called.

"Mr. Perch, I have your document translated. I think it's important that you read what you have signed."

"Why, is it bad?" I asked, nervously.

"It's not my business to advise you, but off the record, you're totally responsible for your new girlfriend. The contract appears to be iron clad. There's a line in the contract stating that even if she leaves you, you're responsible for sending one thousand U.S. dollars to her parents each and every month for the rest of their lives."

I couldn't believe what I was hearing. I hated myself for being taken so easily. "Thank you," I told her. "I'll be right in and pick it up."

It was time to meet with Hugh.

"How is the old married man? Hugh asked as he greeted me."

"I'm doing all right I guess. But I have to show you something." I gave him the English version of the contract.

"I know that you're no lawyer, but what is your opinion of what you see here."

"You didn't sign this yet, did you?" he said while in the midst of reading."

"Yes, I signed the original in Spanish and had it notarized. Marcela has it in her leather briefcase and it never leaves her sight. She now only has to sign her part in front of a Spanish notary for the contract to be completely valid."

"This is serious," he said. "You are completely responsible for her for the rest of her life, even if you two don't get married. She's got you nailed. Why would you sign something so important if you couldn't read it?"

"Hugh, I've always been weak when influenced by strong-willed women. I didn't want to marry either of my ex-wives, and now, I've been pressured to sign something I couldn't read."

"This looks bad," Hugh said, "but there may be a ray of light. The contract is not totally binding until she signs it in front of a Mexican notario, which is a Mexican lawyer, with an endorsement of notary.

"She still has to get this back to Mexico to make it fully enforceable. Can you get it back from her and destroy her copy?"

"I don't see how. She left on the bus this morning going back to the border and return to her home in San Carlos."

"Will, I hate to bear the bad news, but I did some research during this past month. I joined some dating sites online and found her on two of them. She goes by different names, but it is definitely her.

"I am communicating with her myself, and she said that she is ending her current relationship soon and will be free to come to see me.

"I've played along just to find out what I could, and I'll bet that I now know as much or more than you do about her and her family back in Mexico. She wants me to come to visit her in a few months. She said she would be free to travel anywhere with me in the U.S.A. and for as long as she wants because she will have her special visa."

"I had the feeling that things weren't kosher when I learned that she was on the computer all day long. Do you have any ideas on how I can get out of my mess?"

"We have to get her document back before she has it signed and recorded."

"How will we do that? She is already on her way to Mexico with it. I'm doomed."

"Just a minute, little pardner. You've got Hugh Farnsworth in your corner now. I've gotten out of more jams than you could shake a stick at. Get your passport and meet me in an hour. We're going to Mexico. Lucky for us this is the weekend. It buys us more time."

"What is the plan? We can't just barge into her family's home and demand the document."

"That's not the plan, but you're not far off. I'll tell you about it on the way to the border. Now git!"

"I was waiting outside when Hugh drove by to pick me up. While I was inside, getting my things ready, I opened the computer and found that she had failed to erase her history."

I opened her websites to find that she was communicating with at least two other men besides Hugh and me. It was humbling to know that I was being played yet again and the happy little life that I knew was just an illusion. Before I logged off, I changed her password.

My only chance was for Hugh to work a miracle. We drove through the dark hours and reached San Carlos by Saturday morning. We took turns driving and sleeping, thus keeping the wheels turning.

Hugh's plan was made.

From our hotel room on the beach, Hugh called Marcela.

"Hola bonita. This is Frank from the internet. I have a surprise for you."

"Oh Frank, Que sorpresso! What a nice surprise! I was hoping we would meet soon. I have so much to tell you."

Hugh turned on his charm. I could see that he was good at what he did. He should have been an actor. By the end of the conversation, he had her eating out of his hand.

"Well, Will Perch, my job is mostly done. Now, it's up to you to do your part."

I was starting to have hope for the first time since I learned of the scandal. "What do I have to do?" I asked.

"You have to go to her house while she is with me, find the leather briefcase with the document inside, and get it back. You will have to replace it with the copy I made while you were waiting for me. The signatures on the replacements have been changed to Speedy Gonzales."

"Her parents live there," I said. "What if they don't hand it over?" I asked.

"You'll have to get it any way that you can. Tell them you have more documents that she needs and you'll put them with the others. While you do this, make the switch and protect the originals at all costs."

"Okay, I've got it. What time is it to take place?"

"At 2:00 p.m., Marcela and I are meeting at the Delfin Bar for drinks and lunch. You have to be at her home at exactly that time and do your business quickly in case she becomes suspicious.

"You're lucky the family knows you and will let you into the house."

"At 2:00 p.m., I walked up to the door as nonchalantly as I could. Hola, Señora Martinez, it is me, Will Perch, the novio of Marcela. Is she home now?"

"No, she is out to lunch. If you want, we can call her," her mom reacted nervously.

"Don't disturb her. I will wait for her. I wanted to surprise her." I lied. "I have documents, muy importanté, for her. Tell me, where is her leather notebook?"

They reluctantly told me. "It is in her bedroom under her pillow. She said to protect it from all people."

"I don't want to take it. I will only put these documents inside."

They showed me the valise that contained her sacred document, suspicion on their faces. I switched the papers. They didn't see me do it, but immediately afterwards they came after me.

In the brief moment that I made the switch, Marcela's mama had called Marcela at her lunch with Hugh. She must have told Mama Martinez to keep me there in the house at all costs and not let me escape.

"He is trying to steal my papers," Marcela told her mama. "Don't let him get away from the house!"

"He did not steal anything. He put some new papers in your cuaderno."

"Keep him there any way you can! Call Pilar and Alexa to help. He can't get away!"

Mrs. Martinez crept stealthily to me, then walloped me over the head with her tortilla roller, almost knocking me unconscious. Her nieces joined the foray and had latched onto each of my legs.

Blood was blocking my vision in my left eye. As she came back with a second blow, I ducked and she struck her own niece in the head, knocking her to the floor.

The screaming brought neighbors to the door. How could these seemingly mild-mannered polite women become so violent? I banged the remaining niece's head against the table, becoming free from her clinging hands and feet.

As Mama came at me a third time, now with the hot Menudo soup pot, I kicked the bottom of the pot and the hot stew burned her face and arms. She screamed for help.

If the neighbors had stepped in, I would have been a goner. I hit Mama with a right cross that knocked her to the table with her niece. Incredibly, she came back at me, and banged me in the head with a glass bowl that was full of eggs and flour. This woman could not be stopped.

I squatted and swung my leg connecting with her ankles, sending her down to her back on the floor. As I ran across her body which was on the floor, she tackled me like a linebacker. The spilt eggs were slippery and I could not get my footing.

I used both hands to wipe the flour and egg concoction off of my head and into her face, while on top of her. She released me long enough to allow me my final escape.

Somehow, I made my way through blurry eyesight to Hugh's car. The neighbors continued to stare, mouths agape and wide-eyed.

I looked in the rear-view mirror as I sped away, narrowly missing the taxi bringing Marcela back to the house. For just a flash, I saw how her pretty face had morphed to the face of the devil himself.

I hied it to the hotel and found Hugh lounging in the lobby.

"Damn, what happened to you? Are you all right? Do you want me to find you a doctor?"

"No, we've got to go quickly. Marcela figured out what was going on and called her mom to stop me at all costs. I barely escaped with my life from her and her nieces. They're headed here now."

Hugh then retreated calmly to the concierge and asked, "Where is the nearest hospital? My friend has been in a car wreck."

With directions, we left in the car, luckily parked in front of the hotel.

For the second time, in a matter of minutes, I saw Marcela's monster face flash at me from the front seat of her taxi, as she entered the parking lot that we were leaving.

Our only hope of escape was that she would take the time to ask the hotel employees where the gringos were going. If she stopped to ask, we would have precious moments to make our escape.

"They'll be going to the Fe Hospital looking for us." Hugh said. "By the time that they find out that we're not there, we'll be long on our way out of the city. I don't think a taxi will chance following us so far.

"Now that we're on our way, do you have the original documents? We didn't want to go through all of this for nothing."

I felt inside my sock leg where I had folded and stashed it. To my relief, it was still there. I had almost forgotten that I hadn't put it in my pocket. The mother demon witch would have had it back for sure, as she tugged at each one between punches. "Yes, I have the damned thing."

Luck was with us. We had to make a decision to either go off course and stay in a hotel in a pueblo off of our main route or continue directly north towards the border. After two hours of hard driving, we stopped at a roadside taqueria.

Hugh bought us burritos and Mexican cokes. He also paid for a few cotton towels and wet two of them and kept the dry one. He applied ice to prodigious bumps that had appeared on my head.

"I didn't know how hungry you can get from fighting for your life," I said. "What is in this?"

"It's a burrito, and it's filled with cabrito. They were the only ones left. How do you like them?"

"They're delicious. What is cabrito?"

"Goat."

I used the wet towels to clean myself up the best I could. I was sorry that I hadn't at least packed a change of clothes, but who could have anticipated this?

The border guards checked our I.D.s and looked at me suspiciously.

"What happened to you?" they asked.

Sometimes, the truth can set your free. This was one of these moments.

"My future mother-in-law and I had a fight down in San Carlos. She won," I explained, looking the guard in the eye.

He smiled. "Next time, don't make her mad." he said as they waved us on.

We didn't realize the reality of what we had done until we were out of Nogales, and safely in the U.S.A. on our way back to Phoenix.

"I can't believe we did it," I said to Hugh. "I owe you my life."

"You did your part," Hugh replied. "As I told you, this is not the first close call I've had over the years. It might prove to be the most exciting. Besides, I don't know if we're out of the woods yet.

"Hell has no fury like a woman scorned. I predict that you haven't seen the last of your little fiancée."

"My ex-fiancée, thanks to you. I need to make a plan and move. I thought of doing that when I had the bad time with Deena. This time, I'll do it and give a fake forwarding address."

"I wouldn't waste any time in doing it," replied Hugh. "If she's got any influence, she might send a hit man looking for you."

Hugh dropped me off. I checked the damage in the mirror. I had a gash in the knot on my head and a black eye. I still had egg and flour on my body and clothes. Still, I had not felt more alive in years, maybe ever. My adrenaline level was so high that I couldn't sleep. I cleaned up and spent the night outside beside the pool in the pool chairs.

In the morning, I examined the damage to my head. I might have broken a bone in my hand. I would see a doctor on Monday. I planned to tender my notice to the landlord to move at the same time. Manuel and Antonio would help me move.

I knew what I had to do. I was determined to see my plan through as soon as possible. On Monday, I had leased a little house complete with a fenced back yard, garage, and a storage building to house my equipment.

My landlord had become a friend of mine due to all the time that I had been a tenant there. I told him of my situation with Marcela and asked him to promise me to not tell anyone of my forwarding address, should anyone ask.

Chapter 10
Uncle Charlie Dies

My landlord was true to his word. I changed my phone and within a week, was set up in my new location. It had been a while since I had called my poor mom.

"Hi, Mama, how is it going?" I asked.

"Will, I've been so worried about you. I've had terrible premonitions lately about you. Are you all right?"

"Yeah, Mama, I'm fine. How are you doing? I hope you're not still mowing Uncle Charlie's farmhouse."

"No, Will, your old mama can't do that anymore. Speaking of Uncle Charlie, he's on his deathbed. He looks terrible. I don't think he'll last past a week. He's been ravaged by his cancer. He would like to see you."

"Mama, he's just an old, evil man atoning for his ways and trying to get into heaven. I don't think I'll come."

"Will, he was so sorry about how he treated you at Slug's Furniture, and how he left you in jail. It would be so nice if he knew that you forgave him."

I had not been back to Texas in a long time, so I decided to make the trip out there. I was now settled into my new home. I gave Manuel a set of my keys so he could keep the business going and set sail across Arizona and New Mexico.

Poor Mama looked so old. She didn't say so, but I'm sure she thought the same about me.

"How are Gordon and Freddie?"

"Gordon's health is deteriorating. He is overweight and now has diabetes. His temperament is worse than ever. I don't see how Bunny Jo puts up with him. He's kept his job at the factory for a long time. Luckily, he has insurance to cover his health."

"Freddie has moved back to Podunk. He says that he'll never marry again. He has Otis' old job cutting meat at Piggly Wiggly. His dream is to take old Paolo's position someday as head butcher. Paolo is wanting to retire."

"Mama, there are water spots all over the ceiling. Why haven't you gotten the roof replaced?"

"Because I don't have the damn money!" she retorted. "Do you know how much a new roof for a home this size would cost?"

"It seems that a new roof might still be cheaper than a completely ruined house from the leaks."

"Besides, my plumbing is bad. I have only one bathroom left that works, and I can get only hot water running in there. The cold-water pipes have been cut off because of leaks in the lines. Will, this house is dying like I am. I just hope it lasts until I go to meet Jesus.

"You should go see Merci. She asks about you all the time."

"That's a good idea."

I drove the old familiar route to Merci's Taqueria. It was like going back in time. She was still behind the counter tending her business. Her hair was almost all white now, but her smile never changed.

"Que Milagros!!" she cried as she saw me. "How is my little Mijo?"

"I'm doing fine, Merci. It's been a long time, but I've never forgotten about you. How are your kids?"

"They have all moved away, all married, and living in the cities. They have good jobs. I never hear from them. My business is still good. My customers are loyal. Can I get you your special taco?"

"Yes, thanks, make it two."

"Will, I can see by your outfit that you have done well out west. Two tacos of bacon, frijoles, and papas, no egg, coming up."

"Merci, I'm impressed that you remember. Life has been good to me in Arizona, but it has not been without its problems."

"Your problems are always woman problems. My niece in Guanajuato is still disponible. She would make you a good wife."

"Merci, my luck with women has been horrible. I wouldn't want to ruin our relationship by having your niece come to hate me like all of my other women. I'm destined to be a single man."

"Okay, Mijo, have some more coffee. I have to get busy."

"Merci, do my brothers ever eat here?"

"A veces, Mijo, sometimes. Your brother Gordon can eat six of your tacos. He is a good eater. Bunny Jo can keep up with him. It is a good sale when they walk in."

"Freddie eats like you do. That is why you're both so small. He is quiet one. I like him too, but you are my Mijo."

"Thanks, Merci. I have to go away again. I'll see you next time."

When I arrived back at the house, Mama was crying.

"Charlie died this morning. You never went back to see him," she wailed.

"Mama, I'm at peace with how I am with Charlie. When he came out to see me, we buried the hatchet. We even got along."

"He wanted to see you again," she cried.

I dropped by to see both Gordon and Freddie at their work. As with many brothers in their old ages, the mood was strained. We said our cordial hellos and goodbyes, and I pointed my pickup truck west. I was in Ruidoso when the sun went down over the Capitan mountain range.

This time I got a hotel and spent the night. I had never realized what a nice mountain village that Ruidoso was, once a home to the outlaw Billy the Kid.

I had breakfast at the new casino and drove the 8 hours back to Phoenix, stopping only for gas. It was good to be home again. Texas now seemed like a place I had visited in my past, and never my home.

I was comfortable being back at work. My physical wounds had healed. I don't know if I would ever feel normal emotionally again. I accepted my situation as it was.

A few weeks of sunshine and hard work were good for me. It was time to meet Hugh again.

Hugh had gotten a head start on his drinking when I arrived at our favorite cantina.

"Como estas? Mi amigo!" I greeted Hugh. "How are you doing my friend?"

"I'm doing fine. Life has been boring with you back in Texas and with my not being able to chase nookie anymore. I'm just an old man now looking back on my past for any excitement. It sure isn't in front of me.

"One thing is good though. My cancer is still in remission. They tell me if I can go 5 years without a flare-up, I will be deemed 'cured'."

"That the best news I've heard," I replied. "How is the job search?"

"Will, I've had to lower my standards and apply for positions that I never thought I would have ever accepted in the past. Some of the positions don't even pay half of what I was making. Even with that, I can't get offered a job. My age isn't helping me either. Maybe I can be a greeter at Walmart."

"Hugh, Uncle Charlie used to tell me to keep my chin up, and things would get better. By the way, he died this past weekend. I decided to skip the funeral. I had enough of Texas for one trip.

"Mama is doing well but getting old and feeble. Her house is falling down around her. She has always spent any funds she ever saved on her boys. I was one of the guilty culprits sponging off of her."

"Well, don't beat yourself up. People are the way they are and don't really change over the years. She has chosen the life she is living."

It was at that time that a man in a suit and sunglasses approached our table. He looked like an FBI agent.

"Are you Will Perch?" he asked. "I need to speak to you."

"Why do you ask?" I replied. "I don't believe I know a Will Perch." A chill ran down my back. "Do you know any Will Perch?" I asked Hugh. "I believe you have the wrong table."

My heart raced as I thought of Marcela and how she might exact her revenge. My blood ran cold.

Hugh shrugged.

"Well, if you see him, give him my card. I have an important message from his Uncle Charlie."

We took his business cards and I put one in my wallet.

"What was that all about?" Hugh asked. " I thought we might have to make a run for it. I've never met a private detective before. It's scary that they can find people so easily."

"I don't know, but Uncle Charlie died just this past weekend. Supposedly, he wanted me to see him."

"You should call the number on the man's card. It may prove interesting. You've got nothing to hide with your Uncle Charlie. You were nice to him at the end."

I went home and called the number on the card.

"Hello Mr. Perch. I knew it was you with your friend the other day. We have your photos."

"I see that you're doing your job," I said. "Now, what's your business with me?"

"You need to call J. William Schnitzel. He is your late uncle's attorney. He is handling your Uncle Charlie's estate. If you were smart, you'd call him right away. My business with you is over."

The detective gave me Mr. Schnitzel's phone number. I called him as soon as I had hung up with the detective.

"Hello, Mr. Schnitzel. This is Will Perch. Do you have information for me?"

After verifying that I was who I said I was, he stated, "Mr. Will Perch. You are a lucky man. Your Uncle Charlie left you the majority of his sizable estate. You will need to provide us a bank account number for us to wire you funds."

"At your Uncle Charlie's request, we are withholding 40% to be used for taxes and miscellaneous expenses. After all expenses associated with your inheritance have been paid and settled, we will send you the balance."

"You will need a good accountant to help you."

Hugh was right. The call proved fruitful. Uncle Charlie left me over 9 million dollars on his death bed.

He had left his children out of his will.

"The children will probably contest the will. That is what usually happens," the attorney told me.

"And how does it usually end?" I asked.

"Most of the time, people end up with whatever was provided for in the will. Again, I would advise that you speak with an accountant. There will be substantial inheritance taxes to be held out to pay. If you don't have an accountant, then get one. This will be the best money you can spend now. You don't want to end up in jail after such a windfall.

"If you think that you can't spend it all, think again. Many who are poor, and inherit a great sum, will be right back to where they were in a few years, sometimes worse. Also, everybody you've ever known will have a handout: people who you liked and people who you hated. Prepare for that."

"The funds will be wired to an account that you provide. Again, contact your accountant and make your plans."

"My job is done here. Bye."

"Good-bye, and thanks."

I was dazed. I couldn't think straight. If the attorney was for real, then I was rich beyond my wildest dreams.

Now what would I do if one of my brothers inherited wealth? Of course, I would be asking him for my share of it. No, I would be demanding it. This is what will be coming. It may be worth going into hiding."

I continued with business as usual, not talking about my windfall to a single soul. I would bide my time, even in telling Hugh, my best friend.

I did contact an accountant.

"I will work with your Uncle Charlie's attorney for you. It's important that you take care of the important expenses before you begin spending your windfall," he told me. Pretend you don't even have the money you've set aside.

"In a few years, after the dust settles and all taxes and claims have been satisfied, you can get to the remainder of it. In the meantime, you have the other half to play with.

"You are not my first client who has fallen into a windfall. Be careful to spend it judiciously. It will last, but only if you're smart with it."

It wasn't long before the calls began to come in. Of all people, Gordon and Bunny Jo were the first.

When Gordon called me, it occurred to me that we had never talked on the phone before.

"You know that Uncle Charlie wanted all of his nephews to share in his inheritance," he said. I figure that you owe us just over two million each. If you send us a check, we'll deal with the taxes. We owe some back taxes anyway, and our inheritance will take care of it."

"I'm sorry Gordon. Uncle Charlie knew exactly what he was doing when he left me the money, or at least, even if he didn't, it can't be changed now. I'll send you a gift after time has passed. Don't spend any of it yet because it won't be as much as you would like."

"You're the same asshole that you've always been," Gordon told me.

"Gordon, be careful now with what you say. I don't owe you anything and with every one of your insults, your future gift gets smaller and smaller."

Click! Gordon hung up on me in the middle of a loud expletive.

After a while I changed my phone number. Otis was the only relative who had not called me. I continued our monthly phone calls to give him my new phone number.

"Hey, Bro! How does it go?"

"Life is good. How are you?"

"Did you not hear that I had inherited funds from Uncle Charlie?" I asked. "You are the only relative who hasn't called."

"I am the only relative who doesn't need it. I figured you would call me when you were ready," he said. "I didn't want you to think that I would be asking for any money. I won't ask, and if you offered it, I wouldn't take it.

"We have enough coming in right now to buy everything we could ever want. Deena just bought me a fancy Mercedes to tootle around the city with Little Henry.

"By the way, Henry is cute, and may be the best-looking Perch to come along in generations."

"That's great to hear. How are you and Deena getting along?" I asked.

"We get along very well. I'm careful not to make her angry, and she treats me like a prince.

"I'm both amazed and pleased at your good luck.

"What are you going to do with your money, buy a mansion in Scottsdale?"

"No, Otis, that's the last thing I'll do. I'll just enjoy having it for a while, and of course pay taxes on it, and fend off all of my low-life friends and relatives who are hounding me for part of it.

"You know this life of outside work was good for me in the beginning, but it's harder now on my body as I get older.

"I'm thinking of working out a plan and retiring early. I won't get much from social security because I haven't paid in very much."

"Will, I've never known you to plan ahead. The only thing I can advise is to make the money last as long as you can and enjoy life a little more. By the way, I'm sorry about how things played out with your little Mexican girlfriend. I'm not surprised, but sorry."

"Me too. It was fun for a little while and ended in a near disaster. I can thank you and Hugh for getting me out of that mess. My life would have been a cluster-fuck."

"Come see me in my city by the bay. We'll show you around. Got to go now. Stay away from evil women for a while. Bye."

"Ciao."

I daydreamed while I worked, more than I ever had before. The funds were now in my bank accounts. I had spread it around to different banks. It was the first time in my life that the bank employees were nice to me.

I couldn't help myself so I indulged. I went to the local Toyota dealership and bought a white Toyota pickup truck. I thought of my poor Mama while driving it home. A better son would have fulfilled his promise and given it to her. I may do it yet, but for now, I'll enjoy it.

The Guatemalans were surprised to see me drive up in my new Toyota truck.

"Señor Jeffe, did your pretty girlfriend from Mexico buy you a new camioneta?" they chuckled.

"No, amigos, my novia was cheating on me. I no longer have a girlfriend. Now, with the money I saved from not spending it on her, I bought this truck."

"I loved my señorita, but she is gone. I love my truck, and I know it will never leave me. Now vamos a trabajar. Let's go to work."

Hugh was waiting for me when I arrived at the outdoor cantina, already on his second margarita.

"I didn't see you drive up. What are you driving?"

"I traded my truck in for a new one."

"It's strange to see you spend money freely, when I'm having to pull in my horns," he said. "Did your Aunt Jinks leave you her fortune?"

"No, poor Aunt Jinks had no money, and if she had, her kids would see that I never got any of it. There is no love lost there," I said.

I changed the subject. "I want to thank you again for saving what's left of my little life from the jaws and claws of the evil witch from San Carlos."

"It was the most fun and excitement I've had since I used to play around," he replied. "I may have some good news.

"Great, it's about time for the pendulum to swing the other way. Did you get a job offer for that next high-paying executive position?" I asked.

"No, I've decided to go a different direction. I'm thinking about an early retirement. Fate is pushing me that direction."

I looked at Hugh and waited for the punchline that did not follow.

"Can you retire on your half of your divorce settlement?" I asked. "Evidently, you've squirrelled away more money that I ever thought you did."

"I couldn't live here on what I have left, here being in this country. I'm close to retirement anyway and have my pension and social security.

"I flew down to Mexico last month and checked out the condos in Nuevo Vallarta. The dollar to peso exchange rate is very good right now. You wouldn't believe how affordable a home is there. I can even afford a cook and housekeeper three days a week.

"The place I found is on the beach, with a view of the ocean. I've decided to go for it. I'll miss our monthly chats, but the golden years are awaiting me, and I'll spend them in Mexican luxury, gazing at the sea every day."

"Hugh, I'm finding out that there is a silver lining behind every storm cloud. Who could have foreseen that your misadventure in New Orleans would have resulted in your divorce and eventual loss of job, only to be rewarded at the end with a better life? I'm happy for you. Invite me down when you get settled. I promise that I'll come."

"It's a deal. Adios!"

I was happy for Hugh. Some people have a penchant for landing on their feet after a bad turn. He is one of these lucky few. I went back to my work routine, ever looking over my shoulder for Marcela to show her evil face again.

One day, as I was sharpening blades on my mowers, two young men approached me. My thoughts raced as I imagined hit men from Mexico coming for me.

We stared each other in the eye, before one of them spoke up. There seemed to be something familiar in the eyes of each man, even though I knew I had never seen them before. My hackles were up and I had a tool in each hand, widening my stance for an imminent attack.

"Hello, Dad!" the taller one said to me. "It's been a long time."

"We have a lot of catching up to do," said the other.

"My two sons, Benny and Nick, from a life in the past that I had tried to forget, had somehow become friends and had set out to find me. They were strapping young men now. While I was glad to see them, it felt more like a business meeting than a family reunion.

We went inside and I poured them a drink while I cleaned up.

I accompanied them to the cantina where Hugh and I had met so many times for an afternoon of catching up.

"Well, Daddy-O, you don't look like you're living the life of a multi-millionaire. What happened to it?"

"I'm sure I don't know what you're talking about."

"The money! Where's the money, Daddy-O? I know you cheated your way to Uncle Charlie's fortune. You're still the liar that Mom always said you were."

"Is that why you're here? I guess that there's nothing like money, or the greed of it, to bring a family together. Now isn't that sweet? By the way, how are your conniving fat-ass mothers?"

No one smiled.

Benny broke the silence, "Let's cut the bullshit. We know that your Uncle Charlie left you his estate worth a lot of money. We're just here for our share."

"And what do you consider would be your share?"

"We don't want to appear greedy. Our inheritance will be half of what you have for each of us. What we propose is for you to give us one half now and we'll divide it. We'll wait until your hearse rolls away for the other half. Now, that seems fair to us, and you still have half of it to finish living out your miserable days as a deadbeat dad."

"I can see that you've put a lot of thought into your plan." I said. "How about I get back with you? Say, in another 35 years or so? Yes, come back in 35 years.

"Good-bye boys! Go home and make your fortune the old fashion way. Get a Job!"

The men didn't go anywhere, so I left the table, with the instructions to our server to give them the tab. As I drove away, I called to them, "Thanks for the drinks!"

I was saddened as I drove back to the house. It's a tragedy that I missed both son's childhoods, and now when we finally know each other, they hate me and are only interested in my windfall. Life's events do not always have a happy ending.

My landlord was waiting for me.

"Two Mexican men came by asking about you," he said. "They didn't look very friendly. Have you made somebody mad, Will?"

"Yes, I have. I hope you didn't give them too much information."

"I didn't tell them anything, but I'm not sure that they were convinced that I didn't know you."

The signs were all there, and they were telling me to get out of Dodge. I was finding that greed was bringing out the worst in the people of my past. Could the Mexicans have been henchmen for Marcela? Could she have somehow found out about my good fortune?"

I called Mama.

"Hi, Mama. Did Uncle Charlie leave you any money. You were his favorite. I'd be surprised if he left you out, although he had always taken advantage of you."

"No, Will, he left me money in some kind of trust fund. The problem is that I can't get to it. The officer at the bank said that I can only use the funds to fix up my house. Can you believe the shit-ass would do something like that?"

"I've never heard you say a bad word about Uncle Charlie when he was taking advantage of you. Now that he's gone, and left you some funds, you speak badly of him. I'm not getting it, Mama.

"Mama, I never liked Uncle Charlie, but I have to admit that he was smart. Wouldn't the money to repair your crumbling home be the best place to spend it? You could fix your roof, your plumbing, update your electrical wiring and panels?

"Wouldn't you like new floors, counter tops, cabinets, air conditioning? All for free. You could live a better life having a nice place to live."

"No, Will. I like my home just the way it is. I would like to have the money to help out Gordon and Freddie."

"Mama, our previous house literally collapsed from lack of maintenance. You don't want the same thing to happen to this one. This is your one chance to make everything perfect."

"Will, you've gotten uppity since you moved to Arizona and have your own business. I know that Uncle Charlie left you cash to do anything you want. Have you thought about giving some of it to Gordon, Freddie, and Otis?"

"Yes, I'm planning on it, but not anytime soon. This whole inheritance deal is new to me. I want to be careful with it, so I don't waste it. I can tell you now, it won't be as much as they want."

Some things never change. Mama would never update her house, even if the costs of improvements were free. She still wants to give all of her cash to her worthless boys. I was the worst of them when I lived nearby. There are some things in life that defy logic.

"Good luck, Mama. Oh, and one more thing, I wanted to tell you that I may be moving again."

"Oh! that's great news. Will you be moving back to Podunk?"

A thought had just entered my mind at that very instant.

"Oh, hell no! I'm thinking about Canada. I'll let you know after I get there. Bye, Mama. I love you."

"Bye, Will."

Chapter 11
A New Plan

My plan for my little life was coming together. I was ready to move. I had two sons, with a vengeance to get to my new-found fortune, that hated me. I had an angry, vengeful hot-blooded Latina who was out for revenge.

It was time to lay groundwork for a diversion. Canada would be the place of record that I would go on record of moving there to live.

The first big expense I incurred was with the dentist to repair my teeth from the damage in the fight with the Mexicans years ago. I had purchased a new white Toyota pickup truck, and an additional zero turn mower. My workers were pleased.

I took off for a few days and drove north to Vancouver, Canada. I took the long route along Highway One in California and along the coast of Oregon. I stayed in hotels along the way enjoying the scenery and solitude.

Port Angeles was the end of the line. From there, I took the ferry from Port Angeles to Victoria. Victoria is a beautiful place to be in the summer. I would surmise that the winters would chill my thin blood.

I mailed checks to Mama, Otis, Gordon, and Freddie. The checks hardly made a dent in my accounts, but for the recipients, it would have seemed a fortune. I used the ATM's to leave a trail that led to Canada.

I didn't need a crystal ball to know that Gordon and Freddie would blow their cash right away. Mama would hold onto hers and dole it out to my brothers as they asked for it.

They would never think any more of me because of the gift, because in their eyes, it wouldn't be enough. It is enough, however, for me to ease my conscious a little.

It was doubtful if Otis would even cash his check. My duties were done and I had decided against giving cash to my estranged sons.

I devised a will leaving my estate to Otis and little Henry, with Otis being the executor and caretaker.

I drove back to Phoenix on a faster route south from Canada and met with Manuel and Antonio.

"Hola amigos, como esta el trabajo? Hello friends, how is the work?"

"Work is good," Manuel answered. "We make more money while you are away, so next time, don't come back for a long time," they laughed.

"Manuel, I can do better than that. I will be moving to Canada. I am giving my business to you. You can have my accounts, my equipment, and I'll show you how to bill and collect from the clients."

"Why are you moving? Are you sick or something?" they asked.

"I want to live in a cooler place than Phoenix," I lied.

"What will you do for a living?" they asked.

"I will get an easy job. I have given notice to my landlord that I will be moving in two months. You will have to find a place for the equipment before that time and move it there."

"Muchas Gracias, Patron! And good luck. Thanks for everything!"

It was time to visit with my landlord.

"Mr. Little, I'm going to be moving away soon. I'll pay rent for the next two months but you can have your house back as soon as the Guatemalans pick up my equipment."

"Will, I hate to see you go. Will you be leaving a forwarding address?"

"Yes, as soon as I have my apartment, you can send my deposit to Vancouver, Canada. I'll give you a post office box number soon. If anyone asks, tell them I'm there. Bye, you've been a good friend."

'A promise made is a debt unpaid,' I have always heard. In final trek to Texas, I arrived unannounced, and surprised Mama at the door.

"Will, you rascal! I didn't know you were coming. Why would you surprise me this way?"

"Mama, I'm fulfilling a promise I made years ago. See that shiny white Toyota parked across the street? Well, that truck is yours now. I want to trade it for the Corolla. Do you still have the title?"

"Yes, I think so. Let me find it."

We exchanged titles, and my final words to Mama were: "Mama, this pickup is yours, free and clear, to do anything you want with it. I'm asking you to keep it for yourself and not give it to the Gordon or Freddie. Again, however, it is yours now, and you can do with it what you want."

Mama was crying. "No one has ever given me anything so nice in my entire life. I love you, Will."

With that, I took the Corolla to Merci's.

"Merci, I am going away. I will go to Canada. You must not tell anyone where I am."

"Mijo, what have you done?"

"Merci, I have robbed a bank. You are the only one who knows this. I wanted to say good-bye and leave you with a gift."

Merci was taking in my story hook, line, and sinker.

"Here is your gift. Don't open the box until after I am gone. The only thing I ask for is the name and address of your little niece in Guanajuato."

With the exchange of my gift for her niece's address, I was on my way once more. I was growing weary making the long drive to and from Texas.

The groundwork was laid. As far as I knew I had covered my bases. I would go back and see my accountant in person until the business was settled.

I was missing my old pal Hugh. I called him from a burner phone.

"Hola amigo! It's Will Perch. How's life on Mexico's sunny beaches?"

"Oh, there are a lot of sunny beaches down here. I got into an argument with one this morning at breakfast," he joked.

"Hey, when are you coming down to see me?" He asked. "You promised me you wouldn't forget your old drinking buddy."

"I can be there this weekend."

"Will you be flying? I'll meet you at the airport." Hugh offered.

"No, Hugh, that's kind of you, but it suits my plan better to drive."

"I'm sure you checked a map. Do you know it is 1,200 miles from Phoenix to here? Are you sure you want to drive? You would need at least two days."

"Yes, I'll explain when I get there. Give me your address and I'll see you on the weekend. Make sure you have some good beer on ice. My favorite is Bohemia dark."

"Got it. See you soon."

Now perhaps the hardest problem was trying to figure out how to access money while in Mexico. I wanted enough cash to last me a long time. At the same time, safety was my primary concern for the remainder. I would leave the largest part of my money in American banks.

My plan was to draw a large amount of cash and drive it down. It would be risky, because if I was caught with the cash, the Mexican police would probably take it away. But if I could make it work, the amount I had in mind, would last me long enough to figure out a better system.

I arranged to have $250,000 in cash available to take with me. It wasn't as easy as I thought it would be and I had to postpone my trip another week. I got my cash in twenty-dollar bills, for easy exchange for spending.

Each bundle of twenties from the bank are made of 100 bills, equaling $2,000.00. That resulted in 125 bundles. It was more volume that I had thought it would be, but I could handle it. I would stash it with Hugh in Mexico and take what I needed to spend to the 'casa de cambio' for peso exchanges.

I was nervous leaving the bank with the cash and felt like a felon, although I had not committed a crime that I knew of. I had my plan and I would go through with it.

There was method to my madness in trading my new white Toyota pickup truck for Mama's Corolla. I needed a vehicle that was dependable and that would not indicate 'big money.'

I hid the cash behind a fake wall in the trunk of my car. I felt fortunate to drive through the checkpoints in Nogales without incident and into Mexico. I was nervous when I picked up my tourist visa, but the process went quickly and without incident. I would be legal in Mexico for at least 6 months.

My long journey had begun. I was on my way to a new, easier life of ease. I could only hope and pray that my luck would hold out. I almost hyperventilated when I drove through Guayamos and San Carlos, home of Marcela onward to a nearby hotel with protected parking. It was the end of the day, and I needed a place to spend the night.

I checked into a hotel with a protected parking lot. I never saw my room, but slept in my car, just in case I would need to make a quick getaway. Having the cash in the trunk made me a nervous wreck. The second day the procedure was the same after a day's drive.

I arrived at the end of the third day with my two bags after three 8-hour days of driving.

"You're a sore sight for eyes," Hugh said. You smell like you haven't showered in a week."

"Actually, it's been 3 days," I answered. "I could sure use one now. By the way, is your place secure?"

"Yes, it's totally safe. Why do you ask?"

"I have my valuables in these bags, and I didn't want anything to happen to them. Now, where is that beer? I'll be out of the shower in 10 minutes."

Hugh had a nice place. It was a penthouse condo, 8 floors up that overlooked the ocean. He had a large, open-air balcony. It was definitely a luxury home.

"How much did this condo cost you, if you don't mind my asking."

"I got it for $110,000 in U.S. dollars. I could never have purchased a place like this to live in the U.S.A. without paying ten times more."

"It seems like a bargain. Are there others available here?" I asked.

I stayed several days, making sure that my bags were locked in my car during the mornings that the cleaning lady was there.

One afternoon, I contacted the sales agent for the building. We negotiated an agreement for me to buy the penthouse condo next to Hugh. It had the same view of the ocean, but was more shaded, which suit me fine. It cost me over half of my funds. In Mexico, even more so than the U.S.A., cash talks.

Hugh was flabbergasted when I told him about my purchase. "How did you do it? he asked. "I know your yard business was good, but I never dreamed that there was so much money in mowing."

"Mowing is good business; many could have saved enough money to buy this condo with hard work and frugality. However, that is not how I was able to buy my new home.

"My Uncle Charlie came through for me. He was a stingy man in life, but generous in death. I received most of his estate. I'm just as surprised as you are."

"How much did he leave you?" Hugh asked.

"Enough," I answered, "actually, more than enough. I shouldn't worry about money the rest of my life unless I do something really stupid."

My move was another life change. I don't think I would have done it without having a trusted friend, Hugh, to ease me into a new environment and culture where I couldn't speak the language.

It was at least six months before I didn't feel that I had to look over my shoulder lest some angry Mexican woman, one of my exes, or revengeful sons were looking for me.

The days in the sun were pleasant compared to the hard days of cutting grass in Arizona. I would be able to relax and enjoy the final years of my little life.

I went to Spanish language classes with young American students and a few other ex-pats three times per week. I was a slow learner but the instructors were patient, as long as I paid for my classes. Eventually, as I learned to think in Spanish, I could speak Spanish, I learned the language enough to get by pretty well.

A life without women suited me just fine after my bad experiences. I sometimes thought of Pilar, Merci's little niece in Guanajuato, and would imagine having a loving partner to spend my days with. The daydream was always followed by the dark memories of my past relationships and the vision would go away.

Most days began with a walk down the beach for a mile and then back. There is magic in the sunrise on the beach. Occasionally, Hugh walked with me.

Early one morning, watching the sun rise, I became nostalgic.

"Well, Hugh, you've had a good run. Who could have predicted that our lives would have taken turns like this? Do you miss the excitement of your previous life in the corporate world?"

"Not a damn bit. It was exciting and fun, but my life of cover-up always made me uneasy. I could never relax like I do now.

"My only regret now is that I didn't figure out a way to move down here sooner. It's paradise here. I've even thought about changing my citizenship."

"Don't get carried away," I said. "Right now, you have a social security pension that pays for your health insurance. We're both doing well with the status quo. For me, I pinch myself everyday just to know that my life is real.

"Isn't it strange that sometimes the lowest points in life, lead us to changes that result in a better life? It's happened to me numerous times," I said.

"I look back and am thankful to my Aunt Jinks for getting me out of my rut back in Texas. I will always think fondly of my two Guatemalan workers whose hard work afforded me a good living. I can't leave out Uncle Charlie, whom I hated most of my life, who made all of this possible for me.

"Hugh, I've experienced extremely bad luck, and extremely good luck."

Hugh replied. "You're right. The lowest points in my little life, as unpleasant as they were, laid groundwork for change. I don't know how I would have ended up here in any other way. The low point in my life was the weekend in jail in New Orleans, and the events that followed. But if it hadn't happened that way, I wouldn't be here now."

"Providence played a hand in aiding both of us."

We both sat quietly watching the sun warm the sand in the early morning.

"Time for desayuna," Hugh said. "Race you back to the condo for breakfast?"

"You race, I'll walk. I'm through racing."

I walked back to my new home, content now, and counted my blessings.

Epilogue

Will Perch and Hugh Farnsworth lived their golden years in Mexico, in a manner that most men only dream about. Life is not always equal and fair. Some have the worst luck imaginable; others seem to have all the good luck. At different times, the same person can have both.

There are those who have lived both sides of the tracks. Those individuals are the most appreciative of what they have.

Acknowledgements

I am a descendent of men and women who love to tell stories. I suppose I come by it honestly. For this reason, I'd like to thank my family members for giving me inspiration to tell my stories. I acknowledge my occasional bouts of insomnia, without which I would not have finished writing my books.

About the Author

Joseph Hoskins lives with his wife, Gloria, in eastern Tennessee. You may see him often traveling to Oklahoma, Florida, and Italy.

Other Books by the Author
(available in print or kindle on Amazon)

Minding the Store

Misadventures of a Vagabond Heart

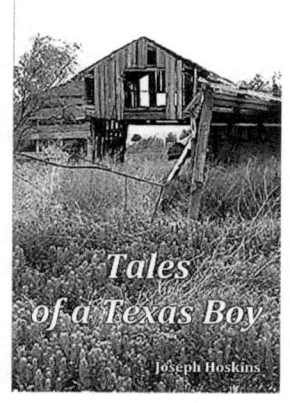

Tales of a Texas Boy

www.ingramcontent.com/pod-product-compliance
Lightning Source LLC
Chambersburg PA
CBHW051453170626
46811CB00002B/462